A WIND THROUGH THE HEATHER
A novel of the Highland Clearances

D1388969

A WIND THROUGH THE HEATHER

JANE LANE

FREDERICK MULLER LIMITED
LONDON

First published in Great Britain 1965 by
Frederick Muller Limited

Made and printed in the Republic of Ireland
by Hely Thom Limited, Dublin

There was a wind, it came to me,
Over the South, and over the sea,
And it has blown my corn and hay,
Over the hills and far away.
It blew my corn, it blew my gear,
And neither left me kid nor steer,
And it blew my plaid, my only stay,
Over the hills and far away.

Old Scottish Song

CONTENTS

I

DONALD MACLEOD'S STORY

OFTEN YOU have said to me, Donald Og, that when at last I got an account of the Sutherland Clearances published, I wrote little about the sufferings of our own family. I had no wish to bring my particular case before the public, lest it be thought that my motive in writing was to have some personal revenge. But since you, my son, desire to hear the tale, I will try to set it down before advancing age enfeebles my hand.

I will need to go back a long way in time. You must return with me through the years to a life you never knew. You may smile at many of our old beliefs and customs, at a culture which could not be transplanted overseas, any more than we could bring our mountains with us here, to Canada. But you shall have it all, both good and bad, and you must bear with an old man's rambling, when I try to describe to you the sowing of that bitter harvest which was reaped in Strath Naver.

Imagine me, then, a boy of nine, lying in my bed in my parents' house in the clachan of Rossal.

I awoke in the darkness of a March morning to hear my elder brother, William Og, moving softly about the room. When I said to him that I was awake, he took the steel strike-light and lit a fir-candle in its holder; and I, lying snuggled in the blankets of my mother's weaving, feasted my eyes on all the mysteries of the uniform he was putting on him. Ever since the raising of *An Reismeid Catach*, the Regiment of the Cat, in 1800, the year of my birth, there had been calls for more volunteers to replace those who had lost their lives in the recapture of the Cape of Good Hope, and at last my brother had got his wish to join the regiment. He had finished his training at Inverness, and had been given a few days' leave of absence to take farewell of his family before setting sail for that strange land; and now, this morning, he was off.

Ach, he was a fine figure of a youth, I am telling you that. It was said of the Namhairich, the people of Strath Naver, that we were the tallest and hardiest in all Sutherland, and my brother was so well grown that he had been accepted as a volunteer at sixteen.

When I woke he was already in his kilt, which was of what they called the Government tartan, common to all the Highland regiments, with a white kerseymere waistcoat. Now he was putting on his brick-red jacket, cut very short in front, with yellow cuffs and stand-up collar, and trimmed across the breast with ten bars of white braid, in each of which was a yellow stripe, a 'worm' my brother told me that they called it. The jacket had flat pewter buttons, with the number of his regiment, the 93rd, under a Royal Crown. I wondered in myself how he could endure to have it buttoned up so tight, and why he must wear a waistcoat which did not show at all. He had, too, a black leather stock that came up almost to his chin.

Now he fastened on his sporran, of grey goatskin, with four rows of small white tassels suspended from red cords. He came over to the coggie of water that served us for a mirror, that he might look into it while he arranged his hair into a knob in the nape of his neck.

'Lucky I am, boy,' said he, catching my eye, 'that my hair grew so fast while I was training, for otherwise I would have been obliged to purchase a false tail.'

And then he made me laugh by describing how the officers must have their hair smeared with hog's lard and dredged with flour, before it was tortured into a pigtail so tight that they could not turn their heads without moving their whole body.

'In some of the Highland regiments,' he went on, 'the kilt is forbidden, as being unfit for foreign climes. Would you believe it, they put our men into tartan pantaloons, that stick wet and dirty to the skin, and in cases of alarm are not easy to put on. And when they are on, they take up damp and foulness, which are sure to be followed by a fever. But, thank God, our Colonel has insisted that the very sight of the kilt strikes terror in the foe. So it was three years since when the enemy fled at the Battle of the Blue Mountain before our famous Highland charge.'

I was up now, and dressing myself, for through the wicker partition I heard my mother wakening the smoored fire with birch billets that crackled fiercely, and I could smell oat-cakes toasting. I remembered then, suddenly, that once during the night I had heard her weeping very softly in the boxed-in bed in the living-room where she and my father slept. I had never known her weep before, for outward composure under all circumstances was essential to the dignity of her character.

You do not remember your grandmother, Donald Og. There had been much talk, I believe, when my father married her, for she was a stranger, a Stewart of Appin, and when she was moved she was wont to exclaim, 'Royal's my race!' But long ago the Namhairich had outgrown their suspicion of this stranger, and they used all sorts of wiles to induce her to step first over their thresholds on a New Year's morning, because she had the very high instep of the Stewarts, and this was thought to bring good luck. 'As high as the instep of Christian Macleod' had become a household saying, and there were boasts about the treasures she had brought with her as a bride. She had a *cuoch* or drinking-bowl with real silver handles, and a great circular brooch engraved with the Stewart crest of a unicorn, representing a race who would rather die than be brought into subjection.

When I came into the living-room this morning, I saw that my mother had taken out the precious *cuoch* and had filled it with our strong potation called bland, made from whey close-stoppered for a number of years, in which we should all pledge William Og at his parting from us. She was at the fire in the centre of the room, stirring the porridge in the great pot which hung from a crook and chain, while my sisters, Laleve and Moir, set out the wooden bowls and horn spoons on the table, and the natural of Strath Naver, Cailein Bochd, sprawled on the earthern seat beside the fire, hugging my brother's pipes which had a regimental tartan cover for the bag. Sutherland was noted for good pipers, and though so young, William Og had been chosen to be the piper of his company.

It was taken for granted in those days that any natural who roamed the district was given house-room wherever he chose to stay, and almost ever since I could remember Cailein Bochd had been in my home. Ay, many a battle I had fought with other boys who teased him, for he was as gentle as a fawn, and as helpless. My mother had invented a sign-language in which we could converse with the poor creature, whose lolling tongue and slobbering lips prevented him from forming words; and he would make himself useful right enough, for he was expert at weaving willow rods to fashion into the little carts in which peats and logs were carried. The general opinion was that he had strayed over from the Orkneys in some boat.

'Ay,' said our folk, 'you can tell he is an Orcadian, for he will be for ever twisting horsehair into fishing-lines, and he will catch the spotted trout, not for sport as we do, but to eat.'

On the clothes-kist in one corner of the room sat my father, poring over the fly-leaves of the Shorter Catechism, on which he had noted down the marriage of Herself, our Chief, and the dates of the birth of her children. I looked over my father's shoulder and read those familiar names, mar-velling again that their owners should be complete strangers to us.

'Elizabeth, Countess of Sutherland, premier Peeress of Scotland, married in London, September 4th, 1785, to the

Hon. George Granville Leveson-Gower, Viscount Trentham. George Granville, Earl Gower and Lord Strathnaver, born London, August 8th, 1786. M.P. for St Mawes, Cornwall, 1808. Lady Charlotte Leveson-Gower, born London, June 8th, 1788. Lady Elizabeth Leveson-Gower, born London, November 8th, 1789. Lord Francis Leveson-Gower, born London, January 1st, 1800.'

I was always very interested in Lord Francis, because he was the same age as myself.

'Pity it is,' sighed my father, 'that the Young Chief could not be leading you into battle, William Og. Well I remember the day when the news reached us of the birth of an heir to Herself. Our hope was that he would be fostered among us in the old tradition, that he might learn at first-hand the problems of his people and their way of life. You mind the old saying, "Kindred to twenty degrees, fosterage to a hundred." But times have changed since the days of the Earl of Sutherland, Herself's father (may his share of Paradise be his). True it is he lived much in the South, but still he would be coming to his castle of Dunrobin for part of each year, and how we flocked to give him the welcome home! Dearly I remember how all our folk would go to him for advice on any matter that was troubling them.'

'Sit in, boy, and be eating,' said my mother to me, 'or you will be late at the school.'

At this lean season of the year before the spring came, I never saw my mother herself take food. 'I have eaten while you were not by,' she would say. And always she was busy. Now, with a sharp eye on her younger children to see that we took good care to conceal our eagerness to eat and so preserved our manners, she set the spindle of her distaff in motion by a smart roll against her thigh, and went on spinning the fine thread for which she was noted, as she took a covert glance into the pickling-tub in which the beef from the bullock slaughtered last Martinmas was almost done, or stood in thought over the chest containing the precious store of oatmeal. Then, in case we should deem her anxious, she spoke cheerfully the Gaelic proverb:

'God comes in want, and there is no want when He comes.'

'Hech!' cried my brother, springing up to give her a hug. 'You will be a rich woman, Mother, with a son in the Army. Every month I shall be sending you something from my pay, which is no less than a shilling daily; ay, I shall send it to you care of our tacksman, on whom the foot-post calls from Golspie.'

'You must save for your marriage with Siusaidh Macbeath,' my mother told him.

He laughed so heartily that Cailein Bochd, who was slobbering over his porridge, neighed in sympathy, and waved his great long dangling arms.

'Why, have you forgotten,' exclaimed my brother, 'that when the Regiment of the Cat was raised, Herself promised her tenantry protection "for all time coming", and provision for the volunteers on their return home? And have I not already received a bounty of ten guineas? Ay, it's famous lucky men we are to serve in a family regiment, raised by our hereditary Chief.'

'That is well said, boy,' approved my father. 'And lucky we all are here in Sutherland whatever. For in other parts of the Highlands, those Chiefs who fought for Prince Charles Edward were proscribed, and their lands given to strangers who, so I hear, are now driving many of their small tenants from the lands they have inhabited from time immemorial. Let us thank the good Lord that could not happen on Herself's estate.'

His kindly face was all flushed with enthusiasm; he could never tire of speaking of clan matters, or of singing the praises of our Chief. Now, while he spread ewe's milk butter on the oat-cakes for us all, he told us again the tale we never tired of hearing, of the raising of *An Reismeid Catach*, or the 93rd Regiment, as they called it in the Lowlands.

'You must understand,' said he, 'that in the wars of the last century, Herself raised the Sutherland Fencibles, who were to aid in the protection of their native land against invasion. They were disbanded when the peril passed, but in 1800, Major-General Wemyss, he who had been Colonel of the Fencibles and is Herself's first cousin, came here into Sutherland to find six hundred young men who were to form a regiment-of-the-line for service overseas.'

'How I begged that they would take me as a drummer-boy!' murmured William Og.

'You were not the only keen one,' said my father, his eyes twinkling with pride. 'For I am telling you that though the soldiers of the Fencibles had long settled back into their pastoral life, there was such a rush to volunteer again that Major-General Wemyss could have had double the number called for. So what did he do but send word round for all the able-bodied men to parade on a certain day, parish by parish; along he came on his tour of inspection, and in one hand he had a bottle of whisky, and in the other a great ram's-horn of strong black rappee snuff. When he saw a likely recruit, he would beckon the man forward, take his name, offer him a sup of whisky and a pinch of snuff, and tell him that in due course he would be summoned to the colours. Our men were used only to the old light kind of snuff, and my word! you should have heard the sneezing of the volunteers when they spooned up that strong rappee! Ach, but they were like greyhounds straining in the leash to be off to war; little knew or cared any of us who was the enemy; we are a race of warriors who through untold ages have been accustomed instantly to answer the call of our Chief.'

'Sharpness to the claws of the Cat!' shouted William Og, giving one of our clan slogans.

But then my father grew solemn, and said it was a life full of temptation to which William Og was going.

'For you will be in a heathen land, boy,' said he, 'where you will find it hard to keep the Sabbath holy.'

'Why, I must tell you,' said my brother earnestly, 'that there being no religious service in garrison except the reading of prayers to men on parade, the Regiment of the Cat have formed themselves into a congregation, have appointed Elders, and have engaged and paid from their own pockets a stipend to a minister, Mr George Thom, who went to the Cape with the intention of preaching to the Kaffirs. As for morals, from the time of the raising of the Fencibles, our regiment has never had a punishment parade.'

'Are you telling me that?' murmured my father, overcome with pride and joy. 'Why, that's a marvellous thing whatever.'

All this while my mother had remained silent, her eyes drawn ever to her first-born. I know now she was near breaking her heart over the parting, but her hands were steady as she set the silver-handled *cuoch* upon the table, and steady was her voice as she bade us all pledge Uillean Og. (Ay, though he was Piper William Macleod now, he would be always just 'Young William' to my mother.)

Still with that wonderful brave composure, she buckled on the narrow white shoulder-belt that held my brother's sword suspended at his haunch, and tied the ends of his watchcoat which he carried rolled up over his left shoulder. She fetched for him his knapsack, bulging with spare shirts and hose, knife, mug, spoon, and tin camp kettle, and his musket, which he told us had just been nicknamed Brown Bess, because the barrel was no longer polished. As we all stood silent while my father said a prayer for William Og's protection, I heard from outside the horn being sounded by Doncha Mor, a poor scholar who received a penny a quarter from each of us his school-fellows for mustering us in the morning.

'Give us a tune, boy, as you march away,' my mother said cheerfully to William Og.

'And what shall it be, Mother?' he asked. 'It must be a regimental air, you know. There's *Hey, Johnnie Cope* for reveille, and *Brose and Butter* for the officers' mess call, or *Fingal's Weeping* for lights-out.'

'Let us have the *High Chief of Dunrobin*,' said my father, 'be it regimental or not. For is it not for Herself and Scotland that you are going over the seas to fight?'

So William Og and I stepped together under the low doorway. He now put on his bonnet, the lower part of which had red and white chequers like his hose, and the upper was of stiff blue cloth with ostrich feathers sewn round it; there was a hackle of clipped white cock's feathers worn over his left ear, together with the black cockade of the House of Hanover. Such a tall bonnet it was that it made my brother look a full-grown man. As we walked down the track, he stooped and picked a sprig of butcher's broom, sticking it in his bonnet, for this was our old clan badge.

Now as soon as ever I got outside the door, I almost forgot my brother, for my eyes as usual sought the familiar landmarks of my beloved strath, my strath that was always the same and yet always changing. There, but a hundred yards from our house, flowed the Naver, river of many moods, now a sleek pure creature sliding noiselessly along, now a sportive little race in which the wavelets refused to go with the stream, but waywardly struggled to reach a backwater, now a restless, busy fall, or a merry spate, and now a deep dark green pool like still death into which all bustling feverish life must flow at last.

There on either side of the river were the two great boulders which, in the dim ages before history began, a pair of giants had hurled at one another in sport. There was the *tomhan*, a knoll of the fairies whom we called the People of Peace. Neil Macibroy, the fox-killer, whom an attack of the smallpox had left blind in one eye, and because of this was thought to be an authority on the People, had smelt the toasting of their barley-cakes as he passed that mound, and had heard from below the chattering of tiny voices as they worked at their crafts.

It was not seldom that we turned up with the plough a bit of strange earthernware or a flint arrow-head, telling of the folk who had lived here and were our ancestors, and often I thought of them hunting on these very hills, and lying now in chambered cairns far beneath us. A bit of such old flint my mother kept in the house to ward off lightning. Many and many a battle had taken place in Strath Naver between the marauding Norsemen and our great Caledonian heroes, the Fiann, of whom we sang about the fireside; there was a great standing stone under which, said tradition, one of Fingal's warriors was buried.

But dearest of all to me was the Mountain of the Maiden, so called because the streak of snow that never melted on its summit was said to be the coffin of a poor maid who had lost her lover and had wandered distraught into the hills. That dear mountain closed my world upon the south, and I had the fancy that if I could climb its three thousand feet I would look down, down, down on to that other, strange world, where lived a mongrel race of men who could not compose extempore songs, or live without food or shelter in following the chase, and who were ignorant of their own ancestry.

It was very strange to me to think that that was the world into which my brother was going now. I did not envy him, not I! I could not bear the thought of leaving my strath. Was ever place more beautiful? I see it now, as I saw it on that bright cold morning.

The leafless birches that grew thickly on the north side of the Naver were all agleam with silver beads, and the mountains were shrugging off their blankets of mist, looking down on me with their wise old faces. Early though it was, the Namhairich were busy, and as always, full-fed or empty-bellied, they sang at their work. The oxen dragging the common plough knew when to halt by their drivers pausing in the song; the girls at the washing-pool uplifted their voices as, arms encircling each other's waists, they tramped the blankets, or beetled linen with a wooden mallet. Every event and task of ours had its traditional melody to sweeten it; the new-born babe was ushered into the world with a lullaby, the corpse was laid to rest with a coronach.

From the clachans of Rhimsdale, Rhiloisk and Ravigill lower down the strath, my school-fellows came straggling after the Boy of the Horn, each with his books strapped on his back and a peat under his arm for the school-house fire. Though I loved my brother and grieved at parting, I was eager to join them, for I had a thirst for knowledge, and especially for the history of my race.

And because of William Og, my mind today was full of deeds of glory, the stricken field of battle, the colourful leaguer, the clash of mortal combat. Grand it was to me to reflect that an ancestor of Herself had fought on the Mount of Battle when Galgacus defied the might of Rome; that the second Earl of Sutherland had defeated the Danes at Dornoch, on their last raid into our country in 1239, slaying their commander with the dismembered leg of a horse, though he himself was sorely wounded; and that another of her forebears had behaved so valiantly at Bannockburn that King Robert Bruce had granted him these lands in Sutherland while he, his descendants, and his clan remained loyal subjects.

Often I would repeat to myself the words spoken by Tacitus to his son-in-law, Agricola, that we Gaels, though a little people, were the bravest and most formidable enemy Rome had ever had to combat.

In the excitement of that morning I had forgot my peat, and running back for it I found my mother standing against the house wall, shading her eyes as she watched her first-born piping his way to war, the red, white and blue ribbons on the drones fluttering cheerfully in the breeze. Her face was as composed as ever, and her fingers never paused upon the distaff, but she said, with a queer note in her voice I had never hear before:

'I have lost a son, but Scotland will be the richer for a hero.'

That year of 1809, Donald Og, lives vivid in my memory, maybe because it was the last one before there fell upon the

Namhairich the shadow of our coming doom. Be patient now while I try to describe to you how we lived in those days.

Ach, it was a hard life enough, I'll not deny it, especially when the harvest failed. We knew plenty privations, but these we accepted as in the nature of things; our racial memory digested them and left us with no bile of resentment. Besides, we were proud of our hardihood, and made a merit of endurance; we were not as the soft folk of the South. Like generations of hunting forebears, we tightened our belts when we were hungry, and this prevented the feeling of faintness; and though life was a constant struggle to keep fed and warm, it was not a cheerless struggle, far from it. The poverty of a whole community lost its sting because it was shared; the want of individuals was relieved, as a matter of honour, by those in better circumstances.

There was no school from spring till autumn, for Mr Macdonald, our school-master, and we his pupils, must join in the annual providing against winter, the common foe. Even the craftsmen of the strath, the shoemaker and the tailor and the smith, and my own father who was a mason, must put aside their avocations to get the arable land ploughed, sown, and reaped. My father was tathing his out-field this year, having let it lie fallow for seven, and once a week I must be moving the enclosure of sod walls further on, until the animals penned within them had manured the whole ground.

The peat harvest began in May, and while the men cut the turf into brick-like shapes with the specially shaped spade called the *torrisgian*, the womenfolk and children must stand the peats on end to dry before carrying them home. Part of our rent was paid in peats, 'a day in the moss' as we termed it, and it was always a merry occasion. For not only did our tacksman send us plenty good food while we laboured for him but, by an old tradition lost in the mists of antiquity, it was a day given over to the wits of the neigh-bourhood, and the sarcastic sayings and satirical tauntings originating at the peat-moss were repeated round the fire-side for a whole year afterwards.

Even little ones like my sister Moir had their share in the busy season; they were taught to gather the material for dyes, dock-root and bilberry, bitter vetch and bog-myrtle, and many another plant. At night would come the ruddy glow of torches as some of the young men threw their barbed spears at the salmon which were attracted by the light, and were now urging their way up-stream to spawn. We of the Highlands would never eat fish willingly, but a salmon, kippered over the turf fire, made a good addition to oatmeal and potatoes in the lean days.

When hay-time came, I was told I was now old enough to hook out the hay with the sickle from among the whins and between rocks, after my father had scythed; not a blade must be wasted, and my sisters would even cut the coarse grass in the woods and carry it home to dry. My mother never seemed to go to bed at all at this season, for either she would be spreading the whole manure from our byre on our precious ridge of arable, or she would be carefully removing the thatching of fern from the roof to gather the valuable soot from it, or she would be shearing our two ewes, or getting ready the churns, the casks, and the kegs for when the young folk drove the cattle up to pasture in the moun-tains.

Ach, how beautiful it was in summer-time, my strath! In June the birds seemed to sing all night long, the air was rich with scent of gorse and meadowsweet and a thousand other wild flowers, and murmurous with bees. When I had been herding cattle, what joy it was, after the silence of the bens, to hear again the eternal music of the river, the cheerful ring of the cow-shackle, the gossip of the old wives sitting at their doors and making dyes or plaiting heather ropes, the constant singing of my people at their toil.

When I came home thus, I thought that not Paradise itself could be lovelier than my strath, so rich and fertile was it, so sheltered in the arms of the mountains, so shaded by giant pines and beeches and the fairy-like birch. A dozen little clachans I could see, each round snug house with its peat-stack beside it, and the byre making one with it, the wind blowing all that homely hearth-smoke into a delicate mauve haze. And southwards, like a bastion, the Mountain of the Maiden would be rearing its jagged pinnacles, depending for its beauty not on colour or on the accidents of light and shade, but upon its symmetry, its awful lonely grandeur between earth and heaven.

When came the first faint warning of what was to befall us? I think the occasion was the *ceilidh* at the house of William Chisholm of Badinloskin.

Now almost every evening in winter our folk would congregate, now in one house, now in another, the women with their distaffs, the men with their tobacco, for those informal entertainments which had been our delight for ages bygone. But this *ceilidh* was in summer-time, when it never really grew dark, and the young folk would be out-of-doors half the night at their dancing, their wrestling, or putting the stone. William Chisholm was not a native of Strath Naver, and indeed he was still referred to as William the Stranger, though he had lived among us nine years. We did not like strangers; those who passed through our land were treated with the most liberal hospitality, but if they settled on the land which was needed, every inch of it, for the native population, they were sure to be cold-shouldered and regarded with suspicion.

Still, we must all go to Chisholm's annual *ceilidh* for the sake of his mother-in-law, a Mackay, whose birthday it was, and she a woman of very great age.

Chisholm had been a smith, and then a tinker, and now chiefly occupied himself with a whisky-still he had hidden in the woods near his house, which he had built well away from the nearest clachan, Rossal. A surly person he was, who drank too much of his own spirits, and who could not carry his liquor; often he had been known to stagger, pure to stutter in his speech, and such betrayals of intoxication were considered by us in the highest degree disgraceful. In so small and close-knit a community as ours was, the weaknesses of each member of it were common property, and because he knew his failing was well known and discussed, Chisholm was always apt to be quarrelsome and on the defensive.

I know that often we Gaels have been accused by our enemies that we were too fond of the whisky, but no agricultural people can afford the sin of drunkenness. Drams we used as medicine, and also freely enough on great occasions, but ordinarily the liquor we preferred was strong-ale. Human nature being what it is, though, I'll not deny that some of our menfolk made Chisholm's mother-in-law the excuse for going to his *ceilidh*, while the Elders and the more strict would stay away. But as I have told you, most of us went for the sake of Mistress Mackay, of whom I had a secret horror.

For years she had been bedridden, and an ugly sight she was indeed, she with her face as brown and wrinkled as one of last year's nuts, and a beard upon her like a man. Fortunate she was, I have thought since, that she was not born in the South, for she would have been sure to be persecuted as a witch down-by. Here folk regarded her with a certain awe and pity, for it was whispered that she had dealings with the People of Peace, and it was well known that nothing good came out of *their* favour.

Her box-bed was in the kitchen against the wall, and she had an uncanny habit of putting out one claw-like hand and feeling at a certain crevice in the turfs, patting it, and meanwhile glancing slyly round with her sunken eyes to see if she were observed. Ach, the various tales there were of what treasure she kept in that cranny! Sometimes, half to please her, half to indulge in forbidden fun, the young folk would ask her to tell their fortunes, or to teach them charms, there being no Elder present to rebuke them for it.

My father began with a story tonight, giving us the one called 'The Darling of the Golden Hair,' and though we knew every word of it, we were drinking it in as though we heard it for the first time, such a favourite it was, and so well was my father telling it. When he came to the part where the hero, Covan, son of the goatherd, must keep his promise and follow the three dun cows wherever they went, and 'they reached a wide moor where the heather was burning, the flames were spreading, threatening to consume everything in their path', the women paused in their spinning with mouths agape, and a shudder ran round the company. We were always mortally afraid of fire.

After this Iain Mackay of Achufrish was persuaded to do the sword-dance to the tune of *Gille calum* played on the Lochaber-trump. He was a very timid young man, and it was always fun to see the sweat start out on him when he came to the rapid part of the dance, his bare toes within a fraction of the two ancient swords crossed on the floor. But he was neat at it, that no one could deny, and never one of those blades did he touch.

Chisholm had his gallon jar out by now, and the drams were passing round freely; some of the young men and girls had gone outside to dance to the music of the pipes played by Hugh Macbeath, the tailor, and the older folk were asking riddles and capping proverbs, until Chisholm, with a high colour in his face and a slur to his voice, began to recite the battle of Fingal and his warriors against the terrible wraith, Cru-Lodin:

> '*Shrieked the wraith of Cru-Lodin on the ben,*
> *Gathered himself into himself on the wind;*
> *Heard Innes-Torca the sound,*
> *Ceased the travel of the waves in fear.*
> *Arose the heroes of Cuhal's great son,*
> *A spear was up in each hand on the hill.*
> *"Where is he?" their wrath darkening,*
> *And each man's mail loud rattling round its lord. . . .'*

Under cover of Chisholm's roaring, I heard Fiona Gordon whisper to me, 'Let us ask the old one to tell our fortunes.'

I knew that I ought not to agree, for Fiona's father, who was an Elder, would whip her if he heard of it, and besides she was a maid who suffered much from the nightmare, and was terribly afraid of ghosts and other supernatural beings. But I was so fond of her that I would be doing anything she asked of me, and besides it was a sort of delicious terror to approach the old dame and beg a favour.

'It is an ill thing to seek for castings on the Day of Yonder Town,' Mistress Mackay rebuked me. She meant that it was a Friday, but she would never call that unlucky day by its proper name. 'Yet I will look into the future, Donald Macleod, though it will not be my blame if it proves little to your liking.'

She went scrabbling among her blankets for the speal-bone of a sheep which she used for her divinations. The bone had been boiled thoroughly, so that the flesh could be removed without nail, tooth, or knife, and then it had been marked off into portions which corresponded to the natural features of the strath. She lay there staring at it for a long while in silence.

It was all just harmless fun, I told myself, crouching there with Fiona on the earth floor by the bed. But I felt Fiona creep closer to me and begin to shiver, and I became infected with her fear, so that presently it seemed to me that the peat-smoke, wavering up to the hole in the roof, assumed strange shapes, as though the wraith, Cru-Lodin, of whom Chisholm was still telling, had come in among us, and that the fir-candles had begun to burn sulkily.

I brought my eyes back to the old woman, and then I nearly screamed. Mistress Mackay had raised her stringy neck and was staring transfixed at the rafters, where a few hens were roosting. Her eyelids were drawn upwards so as to be invisible, her starting eyeballs were red-veined and ghastly, and a dew as of death shone on her brow. She said in the toneless voice of one spellbound:

'Before many years have passed, the houses in Strath Naver will serve as cairns for thrushes; the sheep's skull will make the plough useless; and though the hearthstones will be cold, there will be plenty fire.'

Her aspect was so horrible, her words so strange, that Fiona began to weep. Before the older folk could notice and ask what was amiss, I muffled her in my plaid and hurried her out of the house.

'Ach,' said I, when we were outside, 'the old one's wits are wandering, and as for what she spoke of fire, likely she caught snatches of the story of the "Darling of the Golden Hair" my father was after telling.'

But I was glad enough when my parents came out and said it was time to be going home, and gladder still that we would have company on our way. It is uncanny to be out-doors in a Highland night in summer-time, when it is neither light nor dark. I remember how, looking back at my dear Mountain of the Maiden, it seemed to have the majesty of the dead about it; upon its mighty upturned profile a cloud lay like a face-cloth, and from its shaggy sides all colour had drained. As I looked at it, there came as it were from its depths a sort of hollow roar, very fearsome and eerie.

'The spirit of the mountain shrieks,' muttered one of the old men in our company.

Others laughed at him, saying it was a sound that foretold storm, and that would be bad enough, said they, when the harvest was not reaped.

But my father was silent; and then I remembered how once he had told me that the Mountain of the Maiden was supposed to possess the gift of prophecy, and how he himself had heard it shriek like this on one occasion. It was on the night our old Chief died, so far away in an alien land, leaving as his heir an infant daughter, Herself, who was brought up apart from us her people.

Our short summer died, drowned in the October rains. The stags roared and clashed in their seasonable battles, and a good story ran round the strath of how timid Iain Mackay, returning from a wedding with the whisky in him, had spent the whole night perched precariously in a tree, while an imaginary stag menaced him from below.

The little sheaves of barley and oats had been stooked, threshed outdoors on the wooden platform called the *larbualadh*, and either carried to the mill or ground at home by the quern. The labour dues on the tacksman's in-field and the minister's glebe had been performed; beside each of the hundreds of little round houses the peat-stack rose high, covered by a protecting layer of moss. Our few small sheep, which we kept chiefly for their wool, had been shorn, and the housewives were busy washing away the tar from the fleece, dividing it into carding and combing wool and laying it by for the long winter evenings with the distaff and combs. Each family who could afford it had killed a bullock, the flesh from which was put down in the brine-tub for the rare occasions when we ate meat; and my mother had two mutton-hams, with a row of black-puddings and bunches of herbs, being smoked in the rafters.

My elder sister Laleve, who with other girls had gone tramping down to the Lowlands to earn money by helping with the harvest there, was home again. Strange tales she had to tell indeed about that alien counry, where folk had no music in their ear nor song upon their lips, and thought of nothing but money, where the farms were bigger than one of our clachans, and each corn-stook as great as a house.

The Boy of the Horn announced the reopening of school; and our shelves were full of cheeses, made by the young folk during the long summer days when they were up in the shielings with the cattle.

The Namhairich settled down to the siege of winter. But before it came, there was one great yearly excitement; Hector the Drover returned from the Falkirk sales.

You must understand, Donald Og, that our whole wealth in the old days had always consisted in having a fine fold of cows. With the money we got from these we paid our rents, portioned our daughters, and established our sons. So Hector was naturally a person of great importance among us; every autumn he came round the strath, collecting the black cattle in lots and making them up into a herd, which he would be driving to the southern sales. He was entrusted with large sums of money, and he must be able to keep accounts and both speak and write the English fluently.

But apart from all this, he was our chief source of news. For though he always slept with his cattle, frequented no inns, being content to victual himself with a poke of oatmeal which he mixed with cold water to make brose, and a ram's-horn of whisky, he kept his ears and eyes open, and picked up all the gossip of the fairs.

When he arrived at our house this November, first of all, as usual, he counted out the money he had got for my father's cattle, telling in minutest detail what he had asked for the lot, what the buyer had offered, the haggling that had ensued, until at last they split the difference, or the buyer gave back a luck-penny, and they shook hands. According to Hector, he himself had always the last word, and always drove a very hard bargain indeed.

The money my father put carefully away in an old sporran, that he might take it on Rent Day to the Factor's office. We set little store by coin, for we were self-supporting and had few artificial wants, but of late years Herself had been demanding more and more of her rents in cash, instead of in labour, and a failure to pay one's rent was looked upon by us as a terrible disgrace. If by misfortune any of the Namhairich happened to be short, his neighbours would club together to assist him, or else our good tacksman, Captain Alastair Gordon, would always come to the rescue with a loan.

When these preliminaries were over today, Hector accepted a glass of bland and an oat-cake from my mother, and settled down to give us more general news.

'My grief!' he grumbled. 'I had a heavy journey of it south this year, I am telling you that. There is great talk of what they call the opening up of the Highlands, and would you believe it, there is now a coach-road all the way from Inverness to Aberdeen, which cripples the feet of my cattle, and so I must avoid it, though it is the shortest way and it has been a drove-road from time beyond counting.'

'But why, by your leave, does it cripple the feet of your cattle?' I asked, having never seen a coach.

'Why, you must understand, boy,' answered Hector, 'that there is a gentleman named Thomas Telford, who is employed by the Government in London to make roads, upon which another gentleman, whose name I think is Iain Macadam, is laying a hard surface he has invented, so tough it will stand up to the great iron wheels of these coaches. And would you believe it, the journey costs sixty shillings for an inside seat, and thirty-five shillings perched up on the roof of the contraption.'

'Are you telling me that?' my father exclaimed in astonishment. 'But who is paying for these strange new roads?'

'The Government in London is standing half the cost, and the local heritors the rest,' grunted Hector. 'Ay, and there are to be new mills, bridges, inns, and kilns, though who is going to need them is more than I can tell you whatever.' He hesitated, glancing round at us from under his shaggy brows. 'This only I will say: that though I saw new roads and bridges in Inverness-shire, I saw few folk. Ay, there were fewer folk than ever I saw on my travels.'

I noticed my mother lay down the wool she was carding.

'Where have they gone, those people?' she asked sharply.

The drover shrugged his shoulders.

'It is said that their Chiefs have removed them, and that they have been forced to flit to the Lowlands, or even to the Americas.'

'It is what the packman was telling me when last he called,' said my mother, going on with her carding. 'But you know the saying, "News from the packman and the papers is all lies".'

Yet though she spoke in her usual vigorous way, I sensed

that she was uneasy; and during the ensuing days, I was sure that this uneasiness grew.

I marked it when I came home from school, which was ten miles distant, and I would be telling her of the strangers I had seen in the strath. They had instruments which were unknown to me, with which they seemed to be measuring the ground, and they asked odd questions through an interpreter about the nature of the soil. There was a story that one of them, having lost his way, was guided to his destination by Seumas Macerith, the shoemaker, and that the stranger offered him money for this common courtesy. Seumas was enraged by the insult, for as such it would appear to any Gael.

The last great event of that year was the Sacrament Sabbath, usually held earlier, but postponed this time because the harvest had been so late that folk could not take any leisure from manufacturing their crops. It was the first occasion when I had been allowed to accompany my parents, and even so I was considered very young for such a solemnity. But I had acquitted myself so well at the house-to-house catechising that Mr Macdonald, our school-master, who was Clerk of the Church Session, had persuaded the Minister and Elders that I was ready to be admitted to full membership of the Church.

Though I was proud of the permission to take the Communion, I was daunted by the behaviour of the Namh-airich as we walked the twenty miles to the parish church at Farr. So solemn they all looked, those groups, and there were none of the songs that enlivened every other journey. They walked in silence, or if they spoke it was in low voices, and then only to thank God it was fine weather, for otherwise the more infirm could not have travelled all those miles across the trackless hills. At every spot where we rested, the Elders propounded questions from the Catechism, or made us discuss some point of doctrine. Very important they looked, in the rusty black broadcloth which was laid up for Church Sessions, funerals, and the Sacrament Sabbath.

The ceremony extended over five days. Thursday was the Little Sabbath or fast-day; on Friday the Elders took it in turns to pray and catechise; Saturday was the solemn preparation; and Sunday the celebration of the Lord's Supper. Our parish of Farr contained between two and three thousand souls, and it was like a holy fair with all those people encamped about the little church near the mouth of the Naver. Pulpits of boat-sails were erected here and there, and on the Sabbath long narrow tables were set out in the open, covered with clean white cloths, at which the communicants sat, passing the bread and wine to one another and then, after a reverent pause, rising to let others take their place.

Monday was the day of farewell, and now for the first time folk resumed their ordinary cheerfulness, and there was great exchanging of news. It was often the only occasion when distant kinsfolk met, and there were joyful reunions, a constant shaking of hands, and the sharing out of provisions.

But this year there was an undercurrent of disquiet. The tales and the hints of the drover and the packman were repeated; there were queer stories going round, in which the name of a Mr Patrick Sellar kept coming up. Ay, it was the first time I heard that name, my curse on it!

Who was he? I asked my father. Well, he was a writer, or what they called in the South a lawyer, a strange profession of which we knew nothing in the Highlands, for we had our own ancient and unwritten laws. Also it was said that he was thick and pack with Mr Young, a Morayshire man as was Mr Sellar, and Herself's Commissioner, and that these two gentlemen, with some financial help from Herself's husband, the Marquis of Stafford, had built a harbour at Burghead and had established a packet-boat to sail between it and the north side of the Moray Firth.

We were always intensely interested about the doings of

strangers, but I could not understand why, whenever Mr Sellar's name was mentioned, folk shook their heads and looked disturbed. It was not until we were on our way home to Rossal that I learnt the cause of this uneasiness, and then it made but little sense to me. We were accommodated in the barn of a friend for the night, and, supposing me to be asleep, my parents talked together in low voices. But I was wide awake, cudgelling my brains to remember the Minister's sermon, for when I got home I would be expected to repeat the gist of it.

'I have spoken with those who actually took part in the affair,' I heard my mother say, 'so do not you be telling me it is an idle tale. Of the ninety families who were removed from the parishes of Dornoch and Golspie when this Patrick Sellar bought the farm of Culmailly, some of them there were that went to Dunrobin Castle to lay their grievances before Herself, who, of course, was in London where she always is.'

My mother snorted; perhaps because she was a Stewart, she never seemed to share in our folks' reverence for our Chief.

'And what did they find at Dunrobin,' she resumed, 'but the castle guns mounted and charged, a great swarm of constables, the Sheriff reading something called the Riot Act (which being in English, few could understand), and threatening to send for the soldiers from Fort George to put down this rebellion, as he termed it.'

'It would be just some wild lads who were going to Dunrobin,' murmured my father. 'Ay, it would just be some of those.'

'But what should one man and a few shepherds want with three hundred acres of good land all to themselves?' demanded my mother. 'And that is not the end of it. There is a great tract of hill pasture enclosed near Lairg, and let to two sheep-farmers from the Border, who already have a great farm in Ross-shire. How are our folk to feed their cattle if the common pasture is enclosed, and if they cannot feed their stock, how will they pay their rents?'

My father said something in reply, so low I could not catch it.

'Now royal's my race!' exclaimed my mother. 'I am telling you, man, I come from a people well used to treacherous attacks, and that there are two ways of attacking. There is the open way; or, if you are of the South, there is the entangling your victim in dirty legal tricks. Herself has lived all her life in the South, and she'll have plenty lawyers to cheat us with their sheepskin parchments and their alien laws.'

'A bad meeting to you, Christian!' my father cried angrily. 'All these folk who have been removed have been given land near their former homes, and we may be sure it is good land, for Herself has a care of all of us, her kinsmen. Though she is the apple on the topmost bough, we are all the fruit of the same tree.'

He would say no more; but before I fell asleep I heard him sigh, as though for all his faith in Herself he was very greatly troubled.

2

LETTER FROM PATRICK SELLAR TO A FRIEND IN ENGLAND

CULMAILLY FARM, Sutherlandshire, North Britain. September 28th, 1810.

I am obliged to you for your compliments on the honour recently conferred upon me by the noble proprietors of this estate. The Marquis of Stafford was gracious enough to remark to Mr Young, his Commissioner here, that my having acted as Procurator Fiscal to the satisfaction of the Sheriff-Substitute and Sheriff-Depute of Morayshire, in whose courts I was in the habit of appearing, affords a guarantee that I will perform my new duties as his lordship's Factor with discretion.

As you are little acquainted with this *terra incognita* and its customs, I must inform you that a factor is the functionary who carries out the arrangements, previously decided upon by the resident Commissioner, for the in-putting and out-putting of tenants. Since I am now to combine the offices of Factor for the noble proprietors and Procurator Fiscal for the Crown, my duties must keep me very busily employed; but I flatter myself that my legal training will enable me to bring law and order to these uncivilised parts, a training lacked by my predecessor as Factor, Mr Falconer.

The County of Sutherland consists chiefly of a vast range of very high mountains, dismal enough to civilised eyes, but calculated, both from their natural situation, and from the succession of alpine plants with which they abound, for the pasturing of the large breed of sheep known as Cheviots.

Along the coast there is a fringe of arable land well suited for improvements, and the ocean abundantly furnishes all sorts of fish.

But these advantages have long been disregarded. Strangers are in the habit of fishing along the coast, while the natives live in the recesses of the mountains, rearing with difficulty small black cattle, sowing ridiculous little patches of corn on the wasteful run-rig system, following habits of idleness, and chiefly earning their subsistence from the profits of illicit distilling. I do assure you that to Parliament whisky they are complete strangers!

These are the conclusions to which I have come after farming Culmailly for a year, and by close examinatian of all parts of this vast estate. The cotton-grass in spring, and the alpine plants flourishing in succession if the heather is burnt during that season, have enabled me to raise great healthy flocks of sheep upon the three hundred acres for which I pay the rent of twenty-five shillings per acre, with an advance from the noble proprietors of fifteen hundred pounds sterling at six-and-a-half per cent interest, to assist with the improvements.

Immediately upon my being appointed Factor, I made it my business to call upon the various tacksmen on the estate. You must understand that in North Britain a tack signifies a lease, and that these tacksmen are a relic of the clan system, when it was necessary for a Chief to have henchmen who could recruit quickly, and could inform him how many men he would be able to bring into the field in the tribal wars, and in the unnatural rebellions of the last century. The tacksmen are, therefore, an anachronism, known of old as 'kindly tenants', who, since the abolition of the heritable jurisdictions as a punishment on the Highlands for aiding the Young Pretender, have got leases in writing from the Chiefs, or rather I should say the landlords, in the southern sense of that word.

As it may entertain you to hear something of these gentry (and I assure you they consider themselves gentlemen, as indeed does every ragged, villainous-looking ruffian on the estate), I will give you an account of my visit to Captain Alexander Gordon, a tacksman of Strath Naver, a most fertile valley divided into two portions by the River Naver which, issuing from the lake of that name, runs its course for close on twenty miles nearly due north to its mouth in the Pentland Firth.

I chanced to call on Gordon at his annual 'stock-taking', a most laughable procedure. It seems that once a year it is the habit of his ilk to drive their cattle into a curve of the river; if the place is well filled they are content that they have the usual number, and do not trouble to count heads; they know, they say, how many they need for their own use, and can tell at a glance whether they have a surplus to give to the drover when he comes round to collect a herd for the southern sales.

This is a prime example of the antique, haphazard, and unbusiness-like methods by which these people rule all their affairs.

On my making myself and my new office known to Captain Gordon, he offered to shake hands with me, as is the impudent custom of all the savages here; and upon my demurring, the state of his hands being such as would have soiled my glove, he made me such a look that I began to suspect I had offended him. However, he asked me, civilly enough, if I would please to wait in his house until he had completed his comical stock-taking, sending to direct me such an ill-looking ruffian that I wondered whether I should arrive there without having my throat cut! I must tell you, by the way, that Gordon is a retired half-pay officer who served in the Sutherland Fencibles, and this, together with the Highland obsession with a mythical ancestry which they pretend to date back almost to Adam, makes him ape the grand manner, though by our southern standards he is as poor as a church mouse.

His house is something better than the miserable turf huts of the sub-tenants, even if a sturdy English yeoman would

scorn to live in it. I observed the date 1556 cut in the door-
stone, but presume that this is a piece of affectation, for I
cannot believe that a house built without mortar could have
stood so long, especially in such a savage climate. There is a
garden of sorts attached to it, in which I noticed kale, leeks,
and even raspberry canes, and there is an upper storey to
the house, approached by a wretched turning-stair which
has been contrived in the thickness of the wall.

Within, the place was like a cried fair, full of persons I
took to be the tacksman's relatives, for I assure you they
breed like rabbits in these parts, with besides a host of dirty
servants, all lifting up their voices in uncouth song as they
went about their tasks. A servant lass showed me into the
living-room, saying something to me in her heathenish
tongue which I could not comprehend, but I gathered from
her gestures that she was apologising for the absence of her
mistress who, no doubt, was engaged in some agricultural
labour quite unsuited to the Sex.

I surveyed the apartment while I waited, and observed
that the worthy Captain possessed some few luxuries in the
shape of a looking-glass, a mahogany table, leather-seated
chairs, and a few small carpets. The walls were adorned
with what I took to be family portraits, abominably painted,
and by the relics of the savage age of the clans, a pair of
Lochaber-axes, a villainous great claymore, and two or
three pairs of pistols encased in red flannel bags, all very
dusty from the peats, which, however, were allowed to
discharge their reek up a chimney instead of through the
usual hole in the roof. In a corner cupboard I spied some tall
glasses with spiral stalks, and a great china punch-bowl of
surprisingly fine workmanship; these I suspected to have
been stolen, for the dishonesty of the Highlanders is notorious.

But what really astonished me was to see some books upon
a shelf, and on examining them I found (you will scarcely
credit it) Horace and Virgil among them! From their
condition I was forced to the conclusion that our worthy
tacksman had not only a knowledge of the classics, but was

fond of keeping up his acquaintance with them. This I deemed an unpardonable piece of affectation in one of his breed.

Upon a rude home-made table in one corner there was an account-book open, and I had the curiosity to glance through it. Such a jumble of haphazard jottings I never saw! It seemed that, 'by the blessing of God', he had begun his sowing on March 17th; and there followed such items as, 'Of crocked corn on the short rigs by the ash tree, one firlot'. Intermixed with these entries were accounts of money lent to sundry persons, as, 'To Lachlan Toshach to buy salt for his cattle, five shillings. To Widow Macqueen on the loss of her cow, four shillings. To Iain Dow for his father's burying, thirteen shillings', and so forth.

Whilst I was laughing to myself over this pitiful book, in walks my host, having changed himself into a military style coat at least twenty years old, I should say, with a wig such as I have seen my grandfather wear.

'I cannot find the word "paid" after any of these records of loans, Captain,' said I, pointing to the entries I have mentioned. 'How is that?'

'It would be most improper, sir,' said he, with a high look, 'and a disgrace to the family, to expect such poor people to repay. I am intimately acquainted with all the sub-tenants, and I know very well when it would be right to charge interest on a loan, and when not; also when the word "loan" must be a mere formality for a free gift.'

This he said with absurd haughtiness; but then, returning to that excessive courtesy beloved of all the people here, he begged me to be seated and offered me a dram and a piece of oat-cake. The former I declined, telling him roundly that I had too much experience of the illicit stills which furnish the whisky in these parts, to partake of the same with a good conscience. He seemed about to make a sharp retort, but mastered himself and offered me some ale instead, assuring me that he brewed it himself.

I then began upon the subject of improvements, and was amused to discover that my host considered himself an enlightened agriculturist. He told me with pride that he was experimenting with draining by making ditches, and had recently purchased an iron plough, but though he supposed this would last longer than the native wooden implement, it was heavy, and, 'he did not think the land liked it'— whatever that might mean. I mentioned the presence of a multitude of thistles on his land, and he had the face to reply that he thanked God for them, for otherwise how could he find summer fodder for his work-horses? He could not allow his good corn land to be under pasture.

I thought it time to be round with him, and spoke in this wise:

'In the present parlous state of the county, it is the object of the noble proprietrix to turn the mountainous districts into sheep-walks, and to bring down the natives to the coast, where portions of land will be lotted for their convenience. At the same time it is the intention of the noble proprietrix to introduce among the people regular habits of industry, to encourage the supply of their wants from the bounties of the ocean, to promote the cultivation of the arable land by modern methods, and, while she thus improves the general state of the county, to secure the happiness and comfort of the natives.'

He stared at me in such a way that at first I supposed he had not understood what I said, though I had found his English fluent enough, and not spoken with the honest Scots accent of our peasants in the Lowlands. But then I suspected that he was alarmed for himself; for I must let you know his lease expires in three years time, and certainly he could not compete with the high rents which the sheep-farmers can offer.

'I cannot believe,' he muttered at last, 'that Herself would do her children so much wrong.'

'I must ask you, sir,' I sharply rebuked him, 'to mend your manners, if, as I take it, you refer to the noble proprietrix, the Marchioness of Stafford and Countess of Sutherland.'

He only smiled at this, and says he, with what I thought to be great impudence:

'You are ignorant, Mr Sellar, (by your leave), of our Gaelic way of life. The very word "clan" means child, and though that system has been broken, still it is inherent in us to regard our Chief as our parent, while we tacksmen represent the elder brothers of the clan. Though a Chief may be harsh, still he remains our father; our interests are bound up with his, and he needs us as much as we need him. So it has always been. Our word for landlord is *ceann cinnidh*, head of kin; and I am thinking that to call Herself our mother is to pay her a greater compliment than to refer to her by the grand titles she enjoys in the South.'

'There are two things especially needed in the North,' said I sternly. 'One is the law, for which you have no regard, there being, so I am told, not one single lawyer in the Highlands till I came on the scene; and the other is a proper awe and respect for those whom Nature and the law have placed over you. The familiarity I have observed between the gentry and the lower orders here is marvellously strange and offensive to civilised eyes.'

I cannot think he had been listening to what I said, for he went on as though I had not spoken:

'True it is that improvements should be made, but all improvements, to be really such, must be gentle, gradual, and voluntary, and they must be carried out by those whom the people trust. Years it took Lochiel in the last century to induce his people to plant the potato, now so valuable an addition to our diet. I know of at least one considerable landlord who recently has taken the pains to explain the improvements to his people; I refer to my old comrade-in-arms, Colonel David Stewart of Garth. He measured the arable lands on his Perthshire estate, and lotted to each sub-tenant a portion of what they had formerly held in run-rig, making it contiguous and enclosed, so that the benefits of the improvement were entirely their own.   The pasture they continue to hold in common, but the number of live-stock to be kept on it he has limited in proportion to the quality and quantity of the arable land held by each tenant. The result of such wise and equitable conduct on his part has been a progressive improvement of the soil and an advance of the comfort of the tenants, while rents at once adequate and punctually paid are secured to the proprietor.'

I give you as near as I can in his own words the windy speech of my savage, and I assure you I could scarce keep from bursting into laughter at his ridiculous airs.

'My good man,' said I, 'your idea of adequate rents and that of the proprietors are likely to be very different. But the truth of it is, the Highlands were designed by Nature for a vast population of sheep, and a thin population of human beings. Your glens are cluttered up with half-starved and useless inhabitants. If their wretched abodes were cleared away, a man with knowledge and a good bank-balance could make in their room one vast sheep-walk, which would benefit the whole nation.'

He stared at me as though I had uttered some blasphemy, and muttered:

'God be here! I cannot believe you would prefer sheep to men.'

'I would indeed prefer sheep,' I told him briskly, 'to a parcel of idle and primitive savages who live like conies in a warren. It is as necessary to remove them from good pasture ground as it is to rid it of foxes and other vermin.'

I heard him draw his breath in sharply, and must confess I was a trifle alarmed, for I suspect that these Celts are still dangerous if offended. However, he said to me with his stiff politeness:

'We have a saying here which runs, "So long as your meat is undigested in his belly, the guest must be used with kindness, though he gives you none". You have eaten my bread, sir; and I will observe our ancient laws of hospitality. But I cannot help reminding you (by your leave) of a quotation you will surely recognise: "These men turn all dwelling land into desolation and wilderness; therefore, that one covetous and insatiable cormorant, and very plague of his native country, may compass about and enclose many thousand acres of ground together within one pale, the husbandmen must be thrust out of their own".'

I told him that I did not recognise the quotation, but supposed it that of some agitator. I added that I should be obliged to report to the noble proprietors what he had said.

'The words were written by Sir Thomas More, sir,' said he, choosing to ignore my warning, 'and a greater than he once said, "How much better is a man than a sheep".' He sighed. 'It is not easy for those who live in the Low Country, where so many poor men have nothing but what they acquire by the labour of the passing day, and possess no share in the produce of the soil, to appreciate the nature of independence which is generated in countries where the free cultivators of the soil constitute the major part of the population.'

'My good fellow,' said I impatiently, 'it is high time that your outlook became broadened, and that you learned to adapt yourself to the methods and manners of a superior race, who know infinitely better than you do what is for your good. The inestimable blessing of the Union——'

But here he interrupted me, saying with comical earnestness:

'The whole system of life in the Highlands is so different, that every attempt at sudden improvement entirely deranges it; you would be putting us into the famous iron bed of Procrustes, into which all were made to fit by being either stretched or mutilated. He who rudely tears our people from their birth-place and the tombs of our fathers, may be compared to Aeneas when he tore up the myrtle plants from the grave of Polydore, and saw the roots drop blood at parting from their parent earth.'

You may imagine how weary I was by this time of his tedious quotations and pretence of erudition, and I told him stiffly that the noble proprietrix had as much right to dismiss her tenants, who have no written leases, as a manufacturer or tradesman his work-people.

'It may be true that she has a legal right,' he argued. 'But it must still be a question whether, if more kindness were shown, if the legal right of dismissal were less rigorously exerted, we should see in the South so many combinations against manufacturers and tradesmen, and their houses and property so often in danger of conflagration.'

'Confound it, man!' I cried in affront. 'Do I understand you to be defending these illegal trade unions?'

'I say only, by your leave,' he answered, 'that such a state of society, in which the employed are kept down by the strong arm of the law, and the lives and properties of employers have to be protected by military force and a strict police, does not form a very desirable example for the imitation of Highland proprietors, in the case of the once valued, and still valuable, occupiers of their land.'

At this I could stomach no more, and rose to take my leave. He had the impertinence to press me to stay to supper which, said he, I would find quite civilised, with no stolen beef or illicit whisky on the table (this with a grin I did not at all relish), and where I would have the opportunity of meeting several of the sub-tenants, who had come to him on various errands, one to have a letter written, another to collect the money sent home by a son in the Army, a third for advice on a daughter's marriage.

'And if,' he added, 'you can speak of the days of Fingal, we will have a fine *ceilidh* afterwards, by your leave.'

I told him with some choler, that I had never heard of this person, and that as for staying to sup, I was not accustomed to sit down at table with the lower orders.

Altogether I have formed the opinion that this Gordon is not only an impudent and intractable fellow, but a low Radical, and that the noble proprietrix will be well rid of him when his lease expires.

3

PRIVATE DIARY OF ELIZABETH, COUNTESS OF SUTHERLAND, 1813

July 24th. So cold a day, it might really be winter. Discussed seriously with my dressmaker, Mlle Bertin, how far this rage for being 'well undressed' would go. This was in connection with her weighing my new gown to make sure that it, with my silk tights and transparent chemise, did not exceed eight ounces. Alas, she lamented, fashion had nearly stood still in France since she was modiste to poor Queen Marie Antoinette. In Paris there were even shops for ready-made clothes. Agreed with her that this was most distressing, but privately reflected that it would be a relief to go to the Prince Regent's Drawing-Room at St James's next week, where the old ample Court dress is still *de rigueur.*

Sometimes muse on how the mind is apt to shrink in polished society, under the influence of endless wants and necessary nothings. To live in the fashionable world, we must needs comply with its customs; but wonder occasionally, not without a secret shame, how my fathers would have viewed the fastidious and petty conventions which enchain me. To them, I know, their greatest pride was in a stainless ancestry, and in the fond and close attachment with which they were regarded by their clansmen; littleness in all its forms was anathema to them.

Used once to talk in this strain to George, but quickly shrank from his invariable comments, 'Rude, savage despots; relics of a ferocious age', etc.

At luncheon entertained Archdeacon Bligh who, like so many of our higher clergy nowadays, is a Free Thinker. He rejoiced that divorce is now legalised in France, where, he added, the 'sacrament of adultery' is spoken of in perfect seriousness. Was greatly shocked, but took pains to conceal it.

July 25th. If this were a fashionable 'diary of the heart', to be preserved for my friends, I could not record the distressing scene with Frankie today. But since it is intended for no eyes but my own, to set such things down affords me some relief.

I was superintending the unpacking of his trunk, he having returned from Eton by Thumwood's coach this morning, when I discovered that his kilt was missing. To my enquiry, he replied that he had mislaid it, but he spoke in such a manner that I suspected he was lying.

'I must have another made for you before next Half,' said I.

He turned quite pale, and begged that I would not send it back with him to Eton. Dismissed the servants at this point, fearing that he might be going to say something indiscreet. It was well I did so!

'But you are quite content to wear the kilt at home, my dear child,' I reminded him, when we were alone.

'Only on special occasions, Mama,' said he. 'But at Eton it is simply not done, and it is hard enough to be half a Scot there, without drawing attention to the fact. I had scarcely been introduced to my Dame, when I was surrounded by a crowd of boys who wanted to know my family history. When I mentioned you, they pretended to be frightened, because everyone knew, they jeered, that Highlanders ate children.'

I was cut to the heart by this new reminder of the contempt in which my countrymen have been held since the Union, but I told my son that his elder brother had never complained of any persecution on that account when he was at Eton.

'Georgie!' he cried. 'You forget he was an Oppidan, who had his room in the Dame's House, scarcely even fagged, and only stayed long enough to qualify as an Etonian before you took him away and gave him private tutors and sent him on the Grand Tour. It's very different being a Colleger, I can tell you.'

'Your elder brother being the Heir,' said I, 'had different obligations from those of a younger son.'

I was going on to explain that Europe being so riven with war, the making of the Grand Tour was no longer possible, when Frankie most rudely interrupted me. He was now, I am sorry to say, in a tantrum, and stamping his foot he declared that if I sent a kilt with him to Eton next Half, he would run away and go for a midshipman.

'For I'll tell you now, Mama,' he grizzled, 'what I have suffered from the wretched garment. My very first night at school, my fagging-master took it out of my desk in Carter's Chamber after lock-up, when he and some of the Fifth were eating their supper by the Upper Fire. They made it into a blanket and got me out of my bed at midnight and tossed me in it. And another night, at a Drinkings-in, when all the fagging-masters were tipsy from bowls of Bishop, they got me out of bed again and made me dance in my kilt, while they flanked my legs with a wet towel. And ever since then I've been nicknamed Cold Bum.'

With that he burst into tears, and in a choked voice confessed to me what had really become of his kilt. After one of these ordeals he had spread crusts of bread and cheese rind from the elder boys' supper upon it, and had left it out on the floor all night, where the troops of rats which infest Carter's Chamber had gnawed it into tatters.

Was appalled anew by the conditions prevailing in our great public schools, but made haste to assure Frankie that he should no longer be mortified by wearing a garment so ridiculous to English youth.

'I do understand very well, my dear child,' I soothed him, 'not only how important it is that one should do the right thing, but also what a handicap it is to have Scots blood. You must remember that my parents quited Dunrobin

Castle, their ancestral seat, when I was but an infant-in-arms. This was in consequence of the death of my only sister, Catherine, at the tender age of two. Being unable to endure that castle of such sad memories, they took me with them to Bath, where both caught a malignant fever and died within seventeen days of one another, leaving me to be brought up by my maternal grandmother, Lady Alva, at Leven House in Edinburgh. At eight years old I was sent away to a boarding academy for young gentlewomen in England, where I learned to my cost with what contempt my race is regarded.'

He had listened to me with some impatience, and to mollify him I took him to see the panorama, that delightful optical illusion, of *The Burning of Moscow*, at Leicester House. Trust he enjoyed it, but must confess that I myself saw little of it, these huge new coal-scuttle bonnets acting as gigantic blinkers.

Frankie continued in a difficult mood. At dinner, to which he was allowed to sit up, we having no company, he refused mutton, saying that at Eton they never had any other meat in Hall, served 'naked' as he put it (I suppose he meant without vegetables), except on Founder's Day and Election Saturday. His Papa was extremely vexed by his refusal, forbade him to have dessert and ordered the footman behind Frankie's chair to put the rejected mutton on one side and serve it up for the boy's breakfast.

During the remainder of the meal, George gave us what I can only call a panegyric on the Sheep, describing it as the most excellent animal in existence. Was somewhat surprised, for I always thought he preferred beef to mutton.

In the evening attended my weekly anatomical lecture at the Lyceum, at which several ladies swooned most gracefully. Wish that I could acquire this fashionable habit, but fear that I am not sufficiently highly strung. On my return, spent an hour on my *chaise-longue*, reading this new novel called *Waverley*, which has taken the town by storm. Privately deem it very silly and dull, but must remember to praise it highly at the Duchess of Devonshire's *petit-souper* tomorrow.

September 22nd. Exhausted myself in endeavouring to conceal my emotion at seeing Frankie off for Eton. Cannot yet understand why it is not done for boys to travel there by there parents' carriage, but must crowd into that abominable coach which has damp straw in place of a carpet. The usual swarm of Jew boys with baskets of oranges at the White Horse Cellars, and the usual jocose porter who cruelly frightened all the smaller children with the news that, 'a fine load of birch had gone down to Eton the day before'.

Longed to embrace dear Frankie, but aware that this would have been to commit an intolerable solecism. Whispered to him how tall he looked in his new pantaloons, when he horrified me by remarking that at a certain spot on the journey he would be obliged to take them off and fling them through the window. It was always done, he said. Seeing my unhappiness, the dear child added that he was wearing knicker-bockers underneath.

September 23rd. George came to my boudoir as usual at eleven a.m. to glance through my *Morning Post*, having digested all the twelve columns of the *Times*. He complained of the heat of the room, and warned me that if I continued to follow so slavishly this fashion of extreme undress, I should go into a decline. Think this most unlikely. Try as I may, I do not seem even yet to be able to acquire the more modish habits of the English ladies, all of whom among the upper class appear most delicate, and who can swoon, and weep, and have the vapours, on the slightest provocation.

Since seeing Frankie off yesterday, I have been musing upon my own school-days in England, and I have experienced afresh the bewilderment I felt on coming into a world of quite different values and standards from those of my forebears. It had already been impressed on me, indeed, by my grandmother, that most worldly-wise and ambitious woman, that since the Union, England has had an entire lack of interest in her northern neighbour, once so formidable a foe, and that when I went south I must take care to make myself as un-Scottish as I was able. Success, said she, consisted in knowing the right people, sending one's children to the right schools, being accepted by a closely organised and intermarried upper caste.

I did my best, I like to think, but I still remember how hard it was to unlearn the history taught me as a little child by my Scots nurse, how bewildering to have to regard King Edward III as a hero, William Wallace as a rebel and a traitor, and never on any account to mention Bannockburn. How my school-fellows whispered and laughed when I stood during those strange prayers in church! I had been bred a Presbyterian, and we never knelt.

And even now I find many things perplexing. It is fashionable to profess an admiration for Robert Burns, and my friends are surprised when I tell them that I cannot understand his dialect any better than they can. 'But you are Scotch,' they say. Our own Highland bards are unknown, and if known would be utterly despised. It is 'picturesque' to have Highland attendants; my sons may wear the kilt on certain recognised occasions; but to take any interest in my tenants (I had almost written, 'my clan') is simply not done.

Which brings me to the conversation I had with my husband in my boudoir this morning.

'The success of the American colonists in their unnatural rebellion,' said George, 'has unsettled the Scots. They complain that they have but forty-five Members in a House of Commons of six hundred; and now here are some of their so-called men of letters taking up the cry of the colonists, that they are not responsible to a government not responsible to them. In fact, they demand an extension of the franchise.'

'It is a conception springing from the clan system,' I ventured to remark, 'in which, though the status varied, each man had his recognised place within the corporate whole, and was entitled to speak his mind freely to his Chief.'

4

'The next thing we shall hear,' said George, choosing to ignore my observation, 'is your ignorant Highland peasantry demanding the vote. These agitators never pause to consider whether, how wide might be the electorate, representation by a small minority of Scots in a large English Parliament, would secure the benefits ascribed to a wider franchise. Give every Jock and Donald his voice in the affairs of Great Britain, and the millennium will follow at once! I declare, the new Religion of Man is even more mischievous than the old Religion of God. You saw for yourself, my dear,' he added darkly, 'how the *canaille* behaved towards their betters when they were seduced by political agitators in France.'

I shuddered. Never will I forget that terrible time when George was Ambassador Extraordinary to the Court of France, and we witnessed the beginning of that bloody Revolution.

'Where will this Radical madness stop?' demanded George, irritably swinging my new pier-glass on its stand. 'There is actually a demand to abolish the law whereby a woman's property, earnings, conscience and children belong without conditions to her husband. It would not really surprise me to find some agitator proclaiming the rights of cats and dogs.'

I laughed dutifully; but I could not help remembering that though I have no legal existence here in England, by the law of Gaeldom I am still the Chief, I am still *Ban Mhor fhear Chat*, the guarantee to my people of justice and security. As though he read my thoughts, George said abruptly:

'I have your Factor, Sellar, calling upon me by appointment at noon, to discuss certain improvements on your Highland estate.'

My heart sank at these words, for I guessed what they portended. A piece of parchment and a lump of wax are to be substituted for the unwritten right to land in the Highlands, a right which, though it has no legal recognition and is unknown to the Statute Book, was gained and maintained by centuries of occupation and service. My lands in Sutherland, though rugged, have supported fifteen thousand people, who to George are only useful in so far as they can pay their rents. I truly believe that he regards them no more than if they were pawns upon a chessboard, to be moved as best suits his game. May God forgive me if I wrong him.

I attempted to plead with him. I reminded him among other things of the solemn promises of protection for my tenantry and of provision for their sons, made by me when, as a girl, I raised the Sutherland Fencibles, promises repeated in my name by Major-General Wemyss 'for all time coming' in 1800.

'Such promises were verbal,' George replied coldly, 'and did not tie you down in law. Moreover, when the Fencibles were embodied in the 93rd and became a regiment-of-the-line they were amply provided for at the public expense. The stigma of accepting private charity has been removed from these men, for which I hope they are duly grateful. You must not allow your natural tender-heartedness, my love, to stand in the way of the improvements I plan for your estate, improvements which, I assure you, will be to the ultimate good of your peasantry.'

'I am aware that you know best in these matters, George,' I murmured, 'and I would prefer not to see this man Sellar when he calls.'

'A most sensible decision, my dear,' said my husband, giving me a kiss. 'Fair ladies should not trouble their heads with business.'

But it was not sensible; it was cowardly. I should have seen the Factor. I might have learnt from him how my people were being provided for, whether their ancient rights were being respected. They are so helpless, so dependent on their Chief!

But alas, I might have learnt other things which would only have distressed me, and which I am powerless to avert.

4

LETTER FROM PATRICK SELLAR TO HIS WIFE

THE GOLDEN CROSS HOTEL, London. September 23rd, 1813.

I am sending my man with this to the Post Office in Lombard Street, where letters are received until 7.30 p.m. for a fee of sixpence, not being able to place it in time in one of the post boxes which close at four in every part of this metropolis; for I am aware that you will be anxious to hear of my adventures. As for my impressions of London generally, I will not take time to set them down here, but will mention only the wonderful effect of the streets at night under this new gas lighting. Some complain that it smells, but I tell them laughingly that they should have their nostrils offended by a Highland peat fire before they grumble!

Upon the evening of my arrival, James Loch Esq., Commissioner for the Marquis of Stafford's English estates, was obliging enough to call on me, to prepare me, as he said, for my reception by my Lord Marquis. Mr Loch is writing a book intituled, *An Account of the Improvements on the Estates of the Marquis of Stafford in the Counties of Stafford and Salop*, and he waxed eloquent upon what had been done in those counties under his own supervision.

I found him, I confesss, somewhat tedious, for he insisted upon telling me much that I already knew. That, for example, in the wars of the last century there had been unprecedented prices paid for corn, mutton and wool, and that after the peace it had been possible for the landlords, who are the legislators, to keep up these prices by a system of prohibitions against all foreign produce. Again, said he, Britain had been forced to feed and clothe herself during Napoleon's blockade of her trade routes which followed his threatened invasion of 1802-5. She had done so, only by growing vast quantities of wheat and mutton by the new agricultural methods. With Napoleon master of Europe, she would otherwise have starved.

He then turned to Scotland, remarking that in the Lowlands there had been for some time a steadily increasing wealth in sheep, owing both to the demands of war and to improved transport. For instance, Galashiels market sold in 1775 but seven hundred and seventy-two stone of wool; before the end of last century, this had risen to five thousand stone, and the value of wool per stone had doubled.

'And now,' says he, 'with the new steamships being built in the Clyde, transport will continue to get cheaper. We cannot afford in these glorious days, Mr Sellar, to allow the fertile Highland glens and sweet hill pastures to go to waste for the benefit of a pack of backward peasantry.'

I heartily agreed with him; and he was then so obliging as to give me some hints which, said he, might prove useful to me in my momentous interview with his lordship.

'The noble Marquis,' he confided, 'is a trifle sensitive upon the subject of his antecedents. You must understand that he is descended from plain Squire Gower of Stillenham in Yorkshire, whose son married the only daughter of a Jewish wool-stapler, Mr James Leveson of Wolverhampton. The fortunes of both these families were founded at the Reformation, when the Gowers and Levesons of the day bought abbey lands cheap, the latter family being so fortunate as to discover coal upon their purchase, so that what had been valued at a mere three hundred and thirty pounds per annum, brought to their descendants yearly thirty-three thousand pounds. When this property came into the Gower family, the surname of that ilk was changed to Leveson-Gower, representing estates in three counties.'

He then, with great enthusiasm, reverted to the improvements made upon this property by the present holder of the name, the Marquis of Stafford, Knight of the Garter, Privy Councillor, and Lord Lieutenant of Sutherland, to give him his full titles. Of how his lordship had written several learned works on agriculture, some of which had found their way into the august hands of King George, before His Majesty's unfortunate malady; how he had enclosed the common lands and driven off many hundreds of indolent and useless smallholders, that he might plant vast waving fields of corn to feed our gallant armies overseas. How sternly he had set his face against the abominable crime of poaching; what bogs he had drained, what roads he had built, what miserable hovels he had knocked down.

'Enlightened economists will tell you, sir,' says Mr Loch, 'that property in the hands of a few is agreeable to the good and enrichment of the nation; and this my Lord Marquis has proved by practical example, since the value of his estate is double what it was in his father's time, and he is one of the wealthiest noblemen in England. On one occasion he paid Prinney's debts, and you know they are not trifling.'

This he said with a sly wink, and I was greatly gratified to consider that I had entered a society where the Prince Regent is referred to by this familiar nickname.

'Lord Stafford's marriage to the Countess of Sutherland in 1785,' continued Mr Loch, 'naturally turned his eyes upon Scotland, but she must wait until he had completed his improvements here in England. Now that happy day has arrived. Though he has not visited the estate there, I believe, it seems to him from all he has heard of it a wild, rude country, where all is wrong and all must be set right, a sort of Russia on a small scale, that needs another Peter the Great to civilise it.'

I confess I was by this time so much fatigued by my coach journey from the North, that I was glad when my visitor took his leave and left me to my repose.

This morning I engaged a hackney to carry me to Stafford House, which stands opposite to Buckingham House, the residence of the Queen, on the borders of St James's Park. There is an arched carriage-way as an approach to the mansion, which has a large dome of ground glass atop of it, beneath which, I understand, is the Picture Gallery, one of the most magnificent in Europe, and there are extensive gardens on the south. My eyes were startled to behold two immense fellows in full Highland costume guarding the door, who looked mighty out of place upon so genteel a threshold.

Knowing the curiosity of the fair sex concerning the furnishings of the houses of the great, I will describe to you, as well as I can, the impression I gained of the interior.

It seems it is the fashion of the moment for the English aristocracy to make their houses resemble ancient temples, with a mixture of the Roman and the Greek styles (a mode, by the bye, that assorts ill in my humble opinion with the new gas lighting). Colour appears to have been banished entirely, and the general effect of the white wood-work and the large, unbroken wall spaces is of a solemn and chaste grandeur. Etruscan vases stand in niches, while all necessary articles of furniture have a monumental air, being of mahogany with a lavish addition of gilt and bronze ornaments which, I must confess, fatigued my eye. I have understood since that this craze is carried so far that they speak of a common wash-stand as 'the Altar of Cleanliness', and of a bedchamber as 'the Temple of Repose'.

I was received in the vast, marble-paved hall by a powdered and liveried flunkey, who called out my name to a similar menial at the foot of the Grand Staircase. Thus was I passed on from one to another of these gorgeous lackeys through galleries and ante-rooms until finally I was ushered into the study of my Lord Marquis.

He was engaged in dictating letters to his secretary, and so I had some leisure to observe the apartment. Even the fireplace, I noted, was turned into a kind of shrine, the coals being almost lost among sphinxes, lion-heads, lyres and caryatids. I saw here for the first time during my journey through the great mansion a portrait hanging on the wall. I took the subjects to be the two elder offspring of this illustrious family, Lord Strathnaver and Lady Charlotte Leveson-Gower, depicted in their childhood, he playing with a staghound, while she fed a fawn, a little dog holding up a rose to her completing this charming scene. Above the picture was a coat-of-arms, but I had time only to pick out the well-known cat, sejant, proper, of Sutherland, before his lordship announced that he was ready to speak with me.

He is a gentleman in early middle age, with a large, powerful, hooked nose, very shrewd eyes and a firm mouth. Perhaps it was his dress which gave me an impression of stiffness, for his manner was most gracious and condescending. He wore tight white pantaloons, close-fitting boots, a neckcloth so starched and high that he with difficulty turned his head, a short coloured waistcoat, and a double-breasted coat of a pepper-and-salt hue, with a tall collar and long tails, at present crossed over his knees. His hair was cut short at the back and hung upon his forehead in black curls, which seemed to glisten as though plentifully treated with pomade.

Convenient to his hand was a most elegant crystal wine-jug, containing, I believe, the choicest madeira (or such I guessed it to be from the aroma), a sip of which he took occasionally from a cut-glass bumper to refresh himself during our conversation. Altogether he represented to me the *beau ideal* of a great Whig magnate, the backbone of Old England.

I confess to feeling considerable awe in the presence of this gentleman of such vast wealth, and to cover my confusion I remarked upon the two handsome savages guarding his front door. He smiled and said:

'One of them, whom we call Big Malcolm, was in the 93rd Regiment. Being on an occasion told to guard a cannon on a winter's night, he carried it bodily into the guard-room, saying to his comrades, "I have brought this thing in with me to the fire, for I considered it better to watch it here than in the snow outside".'

I laughed merrily at this tale, and his lordship added:

'But for all their ignorance, these barbarians make excellent servants, I assure you.'

And then he frowned. I hazarded a guess that he was thinking of those far more excellent Sutherland acres, wasted on the kinsfolk of Big Malcolm, when they might be raising flocks of fine sheep to feed our beloved country. That I was not far out in my guess was proved by his next remark, which he made with considerable vehemence:

'More than three thousand wretched hovels defiling the ground, housing a people who speak an antediluvian language no man can understand, who profess a religion no man can enjoy, and who feed their miserable vanity by rehearsing the names of mythical ancestors!'

I trembled before his wrath, though not directed against me, and held my peace. His lordship was then gracious enough to bid me be seated, and setting aside the map of Europe he had been studying, stuck with little flags to denote the progress of the war, he put in its place another plan which I saw represented the County of Sutherland.

That part of it occupied by her ladyship's estate was shaded red, and it was borne in upon me how in recent years it had grown larger; only last March the properties of Gordonbush and Uppet were added to it, and I understand that there is an intention to continue in this manner until her ladyship owns the whole county. Her neighbour, Lord Reay, of old the Chief of the Mackays, is much impoverished, being a confirmed stay-at-home, and so antiquated in his notions that I'm told he has never permitted any arrears of rent to be recorded in his estate books. The noble Marquis will soon change all that, once he has purchased the property.

'Regard it!' my distinguished host invited, slapping the map with his hand. 'Much the largest part of it is turned to no useful purpose whatsoever, and is abandoned to deer and other wild animals, for the climate, at all times intemperate, is bleak even in the best seasons, and therefore destructive of crops; while mildew, produced by the exhalations which arise continually from the morasses, lakes and streams, attacks them continually. This year will be one of famine in the Highlands, as indeed, occurs one year in every five.'

Then he was pleased to smile, as might some experienced general on the eve of a difficult campaign.

'But with the opening up of the Highlands,' said he, 'for which I and other enlightened proprietors have been put to vast expense, the tide of civilisation is now close to the doors of that hitherto shut-in wilderness.'

As he paused to refresh himself with wine, I took the liberty of hinting, as discreetly as I could, that if a road could be made adjoining my farm at Culmailly, I should be the better able to execute my duties as Factor.

'You will see roads cut throughout the length and breadth of the estate, Mr Sellar,' his lordship replied emphatically, 'before many years have passed. For having perfected the improvements on my English properties, I am resolved to do the like for her ladyship's Scotch one.'

He took up a pencil, which my admiring eyes perceived to be of solid gold, and made little stabs with it on the map as he continued:

'The policy I have decided on is to remove, as leases fall in, the population who are passing an indolent and precarious existence in the interior, to the coasts (as near as possible to their former holdings), where education and the benefits of civilisation can be extended to them, where illicit distilling and its demoralising influence will cease, where the people will have other means of subsistence besides the soil and a few starved cows, and where the crops can be fertilised by the seaweed, there nearly everywhere abundant.'

I was deeply impressed by what I might almost call his lordship's god-like charity towards these poor tribesmen, but took leave to inform him that the sub-tenants being what is called 'at will', and having no written leases, it would be perfectly legal to remove them without any notice given. To my dismay I discovered that I had displeased my illustrious host.

'It is beneath me,' says he, very stiff, 'to take advantage of the backward and the illiterate. Due notice must be given, and proper provision made for those removed. On the other hand, the length of time they have held their lands gives them no claim in law; they have possessed them too long already, and must now make way for others.'

'There remain, my lord,' I dared to remind him, 'the tacksmen, all of whom have written leases. They subject the peasants to various servitudes, a relic of the patriarchal system, and in my humble opinion it would be advantageous to all parties if they were swept away, and the whole population be brought into direct relations with the noble proprietors through their Factor and ground-officers.'

I then related to him briefly my encounter with that impudent fellow, Captain Alexander Gordon, adding that I feared he was only too typical of the tacksmen generally. His lordship nodded gravely, and began with his gold pencil to trace a line about the district called Strath Naver.

'You know from personal experience,' said he, 'how well sheep do when the ground has been cleared of two-legged inhabitants. But although a start has been made on other portions of the estate, this most fertile plain is still held by tenants who pay (when they can pay at all) but fifteen pounds for a cattle grazing which they hold in common.'

'It would be worth three hundred and fifty pounds, my lord,' I assured him, 'if it were under sheep. And really, my lord, it would be a charity to these poor folk to remove them. This last winter has been so severe that I have seen with my own eyes a mother feeding her family on nettle-broth thickened with a little oatmeal. Moreover your lordship was pleased to remark, "when they can pay at all"; I am afraid that they take it for granted that in such bad seasons the noble proprietrix will not only be content to forgo some portion of her rents, but will distribute relief.'

I made a pause here, to allow what I had said to sink home.

'The truth of it is, my lord,' I resumed, 'the Celts are mere radical savages, not even advanced to a state of barbarism; if your lordship doubts this, you have only to step into the Celtic part of North Britain and look at them. They are bone idle and disgustingly proud. When work was offered them on the Caledonian Canal, they refused it, impudently asserting that they were free cultivators of the soil, and would not demean themselves by becoming hired labourers.'

His lordship made no comment on this, being occupied in writing certain notes with his gold pencil.

'I trust,' he said abruptly, 'that there will be no resistance to these clearances in Strath Naver. They will be very extensive, and I hear that some of the natives had the impudence to march to Dunrobin to protest, when a southern tract of the estate was cleared for your own farm. One cannot forget that the Celts' hereditary occupation is fighting. Moreover it is a turbulent age; from the beginning of the century we have had serious food riots here in London, while the cloth-weavers in Wiltshire and the cotton-spinners in the North have rioted against the new machinery.'

'I assure your lordship,' I answered confidently, 'that there will be no such insurrection in Strath Naver. The Kirk has the situation well in hand there, and the influence of religion would prevent the natives from breaking out into open resistance of the law. If I may say so, her ladyship made the most happy choice when the living of Farr became vacant, putting in a Mr Mackenzie who, for all he has a Highland name, was bred in the Lowlands; it is in his parish that Strath Naver lies. Besides this, my lord, a very large proportion of the young able-bodied men have answered the call to volunteer in our armies, and are absent overseas.'

'Nevertheless,' said the Marquis, 'recent experience has shown that the women, relying on their sex to protect them, are often the most turbulent and mischievous. I have it for a fact that when a place called Coigeach was cleared some years ago, the females of the tribe set on the eviction officers and burnt their batons, with the result that the landlord weakly allowed the people to remain.'

'With great respect, my lord,' said I, 'the only mischief I anticipate is from the tacksmen. Most of them are obdurate in their opposition to these necessary removals, even when offered some trifling reward if they concur.'

'By a fortunate coincidence,' remarked his lordship, again referring to his map, 'I find that the leases of these lands of— nay, I cannot pronounce their heathenish names, but there are no less than seven of them, all fall in next Martinmas. There will be an auction—how do you call it in Scotland?'

'A set, my lord,' I informed him.

'A set at Golspie this December, and it is my pleasure, Mr Sellar, that you make a bid for all these lands, offering a few pounds more than the native bidders. I will instruct Mr Young to prefer you, and you may rest assured that I will see you right financially.'

This was better than I had dared to hope, and I promised his lordship that I would be exact in executing his commands. He dismissed me with a gracious compliment, saying that by my speech he would have taken me for an Englishman. This hugely delighted me, for you know what pains I have taken to rid myself of our uncouth Scots accent.

I cannot close this long epistle without telling you that before I left Stafford House I had a glimpse of the Countess of Sutherland.

I was being escorted through the hall by one of the liveried flunkeys, when I heard a chinking sound upon the staircase, which made me look in that direction, and there was my lady majestically descending. The sound which had attracted me was caused by the vast number of bracelets and chains she wore; it was plain that her ladyship purposed to take the air, for she had on her bonnet, and a female attendant carried a cashmere shawl and an umbrella, but

I marvelled that her ladyship should wear a muslin gown to go abroad upon so cold a day. I cannot, my dear, pretend much admiration for her costume, the bodice of which was cut so low as to be positively immodest, while her waist was immediately under her armpits. The gown had so long a train that she was obliged to wind it several times round her person, holding the extreme end of it between her finger tips. In the other hand she carried a reticule, shaped like an antique urn.

I stood aside, and made her a reverential congie as she passed, which she acknowledged with a brief nod. I fancied that there was some uneasiness in her countenance, as though her thoughts displeased her.

After a decent pause, I followed and saw her enter a very elegant landau drawn by four spanking bays. I had the curiosity to enquire of one of the footmen whether her ladyship was bound for St James's or Carlton House. He replied with some scorn that had her ladyship been bound for either of these royal residences, she would have worn Court dress; adding that in fact her ladyship was going to attend a meeting of the Friends of the West Indian Negroes, the abolition of slavery in our colonies being a cause very dear to her heart.

P.S. Pray burn this letter when you have perused it. On reading it over, I find I have been a trifle indiscreet, and a man in my position must needs make enemies.

5

LETTER FROM THE REVEREND DAVID MACKENZIE TO CAPTAIN GORDON

Farr Manse, Sutherland. December 6th, 1813.

Dear Friend,

Ay, so I'll continue to address ye, not only because, as a Minister of the Gospel, it behoves me to turn the other cheek, but for auld acquaintance' sake. The harsh expressions ye let fall, nay, the unjust accusations ye were pleased to heap on me at the set yesterday, I attribute to some natural chagrin caused by your being unsuccessful in obtaining a renewal of your tack.

But sair's my heart indeed, Alastair, that ye should think so ill of an auld friend. Ay, so beside yourself were ye, that ye used the unchancy word 'bribe'. In return, said ye, for preaching to my flock that any removals they may suffer will be merciful dispensations of Providence to bring them to repentance, rather than send them to Hell as they richly deserve for their sins, I have been given a bonny new manse, and have my tillage land enclosed and extended. I'll not condescend to defend myself on that score, but I'll maintain a meek silence, as was commanded by the Lord Jesus when we are calumniated. And 'deed, had it been only on my innocent head ye heaped these expressions of high choler, I wouldna have put myself to the pains of writing ye this letter.

But since I was, though inducted by the Kirk, appointed by the local heritor, and since ye so far forgot your duty as to include my noble patroness in these charges, I must e'en take ye to task.

Ye described the set held at the New Inn at Golspie yesterday as 'a travesty of justice'. I canna for the life of me understand what ye meant. The set was publicly advertised; all the tenants had notice to be present; and forbye only those tacks which were falling in were offered for sale, viz. the townlands of Rhiloisk, Rossal, Rhiphail, Ravigill, Rhimsdale, Garvault and Truderskaig. It's true enough that the Factor, Mr Patrick Sellar, bid for each and every one of these townlands, and, since he was able to offer more than the highest bidder for each, they came into his possession.

I ask ye to consider in all sobriety, my friend, what injustice there was in that.

Forbye ye said that the sub-tenants were to be outed from their former habitations and turned adrift upon the world. I canna imagine what possessed ye to think so ill of the noble proprietrix. If, instead of taking so abrupt a departure after ye failed to secure your tack, ye had stayed till the end of the set, ye would, I hope, have beat your breast in humble contrition for so base a doubt of her ladyship's humanity. As I canna allow ye to remain in ignorance of her care for puir folk, I am putting myself to the trouble of quoting to ye a notice, prepared by Mr Commissioner Young, which notice, that none might be ignorant of what it contained, I translated into Gaelic and read publicly in that language after Mr Sellar had obtained the tacks. Here it is:

'Notice is hereby given to the tenants of Strath Naver and others on the old estate of Sutherland, who may become dispossessed. That Lord and Lady Stafford have directed that all the grounds from Carnachy on the north, and Dunvieddan on the south side of the river down to its mouth, including Swardly and Kirktomy, with a sufficient quantity of pasture, is to be lotted out among them, and in which every person of good character will be accommodated. And these lands will be lotted off early in the spring, so that the tenants may enter into possession at Whitsunday next.'

Furthermore, my dear but erring friend, Mr Sellar was kind enough to invite the tenants to meet him on Rent Day,

January 15th next, when he would explain to them fully the arrangements he contemplated.

Och away, Alastair! Is it not lawful for her ladyship to do what she will with her ain? Is thy eye evil, because she is good? Beware, man, how ye resist the higher powers, for he who resisteth them resisteth the Lord Himself. (See Paul's Epistle to the Romans, Chapter XIII.)

I canna help but wonder whether the Lord is not chastening ye for your ungodly habit of playing upon the violin. Mind how often I have warned ye of sic sinful and scandalous levity, unbecoming a Christian. I conjure ye to sin no more, lest a worse thing befall ye than losing your tack.

6

DONALD MACLEOD'S STORY
continued

I NEVER can forget the Rent Day of January 15th, 1814. All through my childhood this day of the year had been a kind of jubilee, when the head of each household in Strath Naver went along to the office of the Factor and discharged his little dues. There never was receipt given or expected; each tenant had his account, and Mr Falconer would just be putting his initials below the sum credited. In his time there had always been a dinner for the tenants on Rent Day, and a grand shinty match after it, but during the four years since Mr Sellar had become Factor, there was no entertainment at all.

When my father returned home on this evil January 15th, I knew by the face of him that he was in some sore trouble. I was mending a harrow in the barn, but he called me into the house, and says he:

'You are near your manhood now, Donald, and must hear of this matter that concerns us all.'

He took a piece of paper from the old sporran in which he had carried his rent to the Factor. It was a dark afternoon, and my mother was sparing with the fir-candles at this season because her stock of them was getting low. I wondered was it the dimness that made my father hesitate to read to us what was written on the bit of paper, as though he could not see it right.

I have that paper still, and this is what it said:

'William Macleod. You are ordered by decreet and

sentence of the Sheriff-Depute to flit and remove yourself, wife, bairns, families, servants, sub-tenants, cottars, dependants, and whole goods and gear, forth and from the said lands in Rossal at the term of removal after mentioned, viz. from the houses, gardens, grass and mills, at the term of Whitsunday, May 26th next, and from the arable land under crop at the separation of the crop, 1814, from the ground.'

My mother and my sister Laleve were sitting on the ground opposite each other, grinding corn. I saw how the stick with which they turned the upper stone became clutched rigid in my mother's hand as my father read this paper, and how Laleve, not attending to her task, kept pouring grain through the central opening, until our precious oats spilled over on the floor.

'You went prepared to offer an increase in your rent, man,' my mother said in a low voice.

'I did,' said he, 'but not from five shillings to five guineas. That is what Mr Sellar was demanding of me.'

They looked at one another, and I knew what they were thinking. William Og had been sending money home to us regularly ever since he went away to war, always ready to go on a fatigue if he might earn a little extra and, so we suspected, shunning the mirthful band in camp that he might add another sixpence to his hoard to remit home. I saw my mother make a half gesture towards the old cheese-press where she kept this treasure; but my father shook his head.

'That money must be saved for William Og himself,' said he, 'when he returns and will be wedding his faithful Siusaidh. Besides, I would take shame on me to be paying so unjust a rent, when all my neighbours must flit. Mr Sellar will allow a few, a very few, to remain to work under his head-shepherd, but from eighty-five thousand acres of tillage and pasture the rest of us must be gone.'

'Now royal's my race!' my mother cried with passion. 'Have the Namhairich become craven that they will submit tamely to such treatment? Do they not fear that the shades of their valiant ancestors will reproach them when they ride by on the clouds of the storm?'

'Whist, woman,' my father rebuked her. 'What is being done is by Herself's authority, and though it is a sore hardship that we must leave our native earth, we must just be putting up with it. Herself has made provision for us; we are to have lands lotted in the spring. And still when my time comes to go on the Great Journey, I may be carried to our dear churchyard at Achness and laid among my forebears.'

It was ever the same with my father. It was not that he lacked spirit, but he could no more think of disobeying his Chief than of flouting the stern ordinances of God. And always he would be finding some excuse for Herself. Left an orphan in her infancy, sad pity it was, he would say, that she had no *tuit-fhear*, no guardian uncle, to manage clan affairs for her, but only wealthy dukes and earls of the South.

I think now, looking back, that there was in all the Namhairich an inability to believe that this could happen to them, though what had been done elsewhere on the estate and indeed throughout the Highlands should have warned them. Only my father and Mr Iain Gordon, the Elder, made preparations for departure, selling off most of their cattle which, in that lean season of the year, fetched next to nothing, that they might have a little money in hand and also because they could not support so many head of cows upon the two acres which was all the Namhairich were to have in their new homes.

The other folk went about their affairs as though no threat of eviction was hanging over them. Mr Gordon gravely rebuked them for their presumption; they were tempting the Lord, said he, by this undue confidence that they would be allowed to remain. They in their turn were shocked by the independent action of my father and Mr Gordon, for in all matters it was customary to act as a community; and they were encouraged in this attitude by Mr Sage, the good minister of Kildonan.

It was he who sometimes preached at our Mission House, and he rigorously dissented from the parrot cry of all the other seventeen ministers in Sutherland, that 'God had a controversy with the people for their sins'. He assured us that, on the contrary, the Lord would never permit this injustice to poor people, and he called it boldly by its right name— avarice on the part of the noble proprietors. Besides, said he, though a land surveyor had arrived to examine the ground for the new allotments, this gentleman had been obliged to return home to his sick wife, so that no land had been lotted according to the promise, and our folk had nowhere to go whatever.

On a day in March I stayed late at the school, for kind Mr Macdonald was giving me extra tuition free, because he said I was going to be a good classic, and he hoped I would win a bursary to take me to St Andrew's. As I made my way homewards, I saw in the distance a fire flickering low upon the ground. There was much smoke, but I made out through it other burning points, and fear came on me, for I had never forgotten what the old woman, Chisholm's mother-in-law, had said when she had looked into the future at the *ceilidh* long ago.

When I got home, I told my father what I had seen.

'Ach,' said he, 'likely it would just be some of the young men burning the water for salmon.'

'Or maybe the folk down-by are lighting bonfires for some victory in the war,' said Laleve.

But soon Iain Mackay of Achufrish told us plainly what the burning meant. He was one of the very few who had been given permission to remain, because, being timid and sub-missive, he had accepted the post of under-shepherd to the Factor, ay, and was paid ten pounds a year, with five bolls of meal thrown in.

'They are burning the heath,' says Iain, 'to clean the ground for sheep.'

Now this was terrible news, for in the lean season of the year our cattle, which would eat anything, depended solely on the heather until they could get a good bite at the new grass springing up among its roots.

'To clean the ground for sheep, and to drive men out!' my mother cried in her vigorous way. And then she went at my father to resist the Sheriff's officers if they came to remove him forcibly. But nothing could induce him to commit such an act of rebellion against Herself, even though because of the burning we were obliged to feed our remaining cows on potatoes and seed corn.

Whitsunday passed, and folk took heart, saying that Mr Sage was in the right of it, and that they would not be removed after all. The young folk began the yearly migration to the shieling-huts, my sister Laleve took young Moir with her to earn money at the Lowland hay-cutting, and the rest of the Namhairich were busy with their early summer tasks. But on June 4th all received notice that the new allotments were ready, and that we must be gone within ten days.

Still the Namhairich just could not believe it. Some were even rethatching their houses, as though they were to remain in them another ten years; the hay was cut and the peat stacked as usual, the few young men left in the strath went off into the mountains to get the first vension, and children were kept busy weeding among the growing barley and oats. Only this year there was no dancing and wrestling after work was done, and though we sang the traditional songs at our labour, it seemed to me that each tune sounded like a lament.

My father had laid by his masonry work, and as I smeared our two ewes with tar and fat to kill the parasites, I watched him dismantling our home, a terrible sight to me whatever. Ochon, I felt as though it were the very skin of my body that was being stripped away.

Now I must make known to you, Donald Og, that in those days we built our houses with two kinds of wood. There were the couples taken from the birch trees which, fixed into the ground, arched over from the opposite sides and were secured at their meeting with wooden pegs. This was what was called the upland timber, and it belonged to the landlord. But the ancient moss-fir dug from the peat-bogs, dry, tough and resinous wood, belonged to the tenant by immemorial right. It was used for the battens which were placed lengthwise from couple to couple and supported the thatch of fern. A great number of these battens were needed for a home, and they were accounted one of the few indispensable possessions of a married man.

It was these same precious boards that my father was dismantling, that he might carry them away with him to build another home. Law-abiding as he was, he would not take the couples, saying that these must be left for the in-coming tenant.

Our friends and kinsfolk sometimes assembled to watch my father as he toiled with dogged patience at so grim a task. Some laughed at him for being so foolish, while others asked him where his courage had gone. Martuinn Don, the smith's son, taunted me, calling my father another Fluathas, the coward who fled from his own shadow, and I fought Martuinn for it, while the other boys gathered round, calling out as usual, 'Let them have the fair combat of Fingal!'; and I beat Martuinn soundly, giving him a bloody nose and sending him howling from the scene of battle. This comforted me somewhat in my bewilderment and sadness, for Martuinn was two years my senior, and a doughty champion with his fists.

My mother tightened her proud lips when she heard the neighbours gossiping, but never a word did she say, loyally helping her man. Only once, when we were alone, I heard her warn him thus:

'They tell me that a wolf is the crest of the Marquis of Stafford. Mind you our old proverb, Uillean, "He is a foolish man who thinks he can appease a wolf".'

It was on a Monday that my father purposed to make the removal to the inferior croft lotted to him in Aird-an-Casgaich, ten miles away at the foot of the strath. By Saturday night our dear home looked melancholy indeed, for no work must be done on the Sabbath, and the battens had all been taken down, the thatch removed, and we dwelt under the open sky. The brine-tub and the scrubbed board on which oat-cakes were prepared, our kists for meal and clothes and fir-candles, our heather brushes and farm implements, our last mutton-ham and cheeses, all were strapped up ready to be loaded on our two shelties or carried in creels on our backs when Monday dawned.

Only the great pot fastened on a hook and chain over the fire was still in its place for our porridge, and the Shorter Catechism had been kept out, from which my father would ask questions on the Sabbath evening. Next day we went as usual to our Mission House at Achness, beside the water-fall that gave the place its name.

You would think it a poor little place right enough, Donald Og, seeing the fine churches we have built here in Canada. There were no seats except for a few upturned butter-kegs near the wall for those who were too infirm to stand during the praying; only the tacksman had a pew, with a wooden canopy carved with his coat-of-arms in an escutcheon. There being no Gaelic Scriptures then, the Minister translated from the English version as he went along, sometimes referring to Bedell's Irish Bible. When we had Mr Sage for preacher, he gave us a Gaelic sermon, but on this Sabbath it was Mr Mackenzie, who was a great one for standing in well with the General Assembly, and they at that time were encouraging all Highland ministers to preach in English, saying that our own language was 'uncouth' and encouraged us in our independence of spirit.

From time to time the bell tolled, and groups would be approaching the church through the birch woods, both men and women in plaids of our dark green tartan, the matrons in high white curches, the girls with hair neatly braided in front and bound about by the snood. When I look back upon that morning, there is one young figure clearest in my mind. I see Fiona Gordon, in her best blue homespun petti-coat and clean white jacket, and I can smell the sweet scent

of her dark hair which she washed in a decoction of young
birch buds.

I think that on this sad Sabbath, even Mr Mackenzie was
troubled in his mind, for the first psalm he gave out was the
42nd, and his voice had a bit of a tremor in it as he read the
first few lines from the old version of the rhythmical para-
phrase. When Mr Macdonald, who was Preceptor, had
risen and called out the tune, 'Hundred and fifteen', and
had started us off with the tuning-fork, I felt the tears
scalding my throat, for that psalm might have been written
for the Namhairich, to whom, as to all our Gaelic race,
want of confidence in God was accounted a dreadful sin.
You know well how it goes:

> *'O why art thou cast down, my soul?*
> *Why, thus with grief opprest,*
> *Art thou disquieted in me?*
> *In God still hope and rest:*
> *For yet I know I shall Him praise,*
> *Who graciously to me*
> *The health is of my countenance,*
> *Yea, mine own God is He.'*

After the psalm we rose for the Minister's extempore
prayer, and while he was at it there was a stir at the back of
the church and an unseemly barking of dogs. Who should
come in but Mr Sellar and his head-shepherd, John Dryden,
a Lowlander, who wore the grey plaid common to his
calling in the South, and who brought his collies into the
church with him. Up they stalked to Captain Gordon's old
pew, where they sat themselves down, Dryden whacking
at his dogs with his crook, which only made them bark the
louder. We could not believe our eyes or ears, and when the
sermon began the old wives even forgot to spoon up their
snuff, so astonished were they at the presence of the Factor
and his shepherd.

Now in those days, my son (it is very different now, alas), we had none of the interminable theological wrangling beloved of the Lowlands. Our awareness of God was profound, but our religion was more of the heart than of the head, and we still had some traces of that innocent Nature-worship which dies hard among the mountains. Even before the early introduction of Christianity into Gaeldom, the heroes of whom our bards sang had bequeathed to us high ideals; mercy to the fallen, hospitality to strangers, fairness in fight, the sanctity of an oath. It was easy for our fore-fathers to accept the Christian doctrine; for instance, the immortality of the soul, as brought to light in the Gospel, was for them a glad confirmation of their ancient belief in that separate state in which the apparitions of dead heroes often appeared to cheer and strengthen them.

All this being so, the sermons to which we were accustomed were simple and good, suited to a devout congregation, and our ministers would often work into their preaching some general news about the great world, newspapers being so rare among us.

But on this Sabbath we had another kind of sermon from Mr Mackenzie. Maybe it was because of the presence of the Factor, but my grief! how the Minister did chastise us with his tongue! We were like the Israelites of old, he told us, who had turned away to worship idols; and then he descended to particulars, calling the offending persons by their names.

Sine Matheson, he thundered, professed to cure toothache and warts by a charm (and true enough she did, but, good soul, she never would be taking a penny in payment, always repeating the Gospel words, 'Freely ye have received, freely give'). Margaret Mackay told fortunes; in several houses at the New Year the old superstition of burning juniper to ward off cattle-plague had been revived; and with his own hand he had torn down a fox's mask which Murdoch Mackay had nailed over his stables to protect his shelties from an evil power. Paganism and Popery had crept back among us; and was it any wonder, then, roared the Minister, that the

Lord had unloosed the arrows of His wrath against the Namhairich, driving them out into the desert for their sins?

He did not accuse us, you notice, of such sins as unchastity or dishonesty, for indeed at that time they were held by us as terrible disgraces to the whole clan and were very rare indeed.

But, Mr Mackenzie concluded, he had prayed for us that the Lord would shorten His arm, and if we would repent in sackcloth and ashes, and bow our necks meekly, though we must leave the land of our fathers, we might yet escape the brimstone of the Burning Pit.

I was angry as I listened, for it seemed to me a sort of blasphemy to have the heavy guilt of landlords settled upon my God, and that by His servant who had got a fine new manse built as a reward for persuading his poor flock to flit peaceably. Besides, it was not honest in him, for he was quite accustomed to the fact that we mountain folk had our little harmless superstitions, and were not one whit the worse Christians for them. For that matter, he was not entirely free from them himself; I have known him very vexed if someone called after him so that he turned his head when he set out on a journey, for that was considered a very un-lucky thing to do.

Several times during this fiery sermon, I observed Mr Sellar glance about him at the congregation, and then he would be whispering to Dryden, as though he asked who certain persons were.

After service in the old days it had always been the custom for our tacksman to linger in the churchyard to shake hands and to have a word with the sub-tenants. We waited there this morning, wondering would Mr Sellar, who had outed Captain Gordon from his tack, do the same. The Elder, Mr Gordon, said to his neighbours that now they had heard plainly that they must remove, but Hugh Macbeath argued that often before the Minister had given us news which had proved false. Had he not declared, during the invasion scare, that Napoleon had actually landed? Others had not understood one word of the sermon, it being in the English.

Meanwhile I and some of the other boys were at our usual Sabbath diversion of trying to lift the *clach-cuid-fir*, the Stone of Strength, in the churchyard, and place it on another four feet high. He who could perform this feat was reckoned as having reached his manhood. I had just begun to lift the stone, when I heard Mr Sellar's voice raised roughly.

'William Chisholm,' says he, 'you have been pointed out to me as one who never had any right to land in Strath Naver. You are but a squatter, and you are not to be allowed to remain anywhere on the estate.'

We all stood silent, wondering would Chisholm use any violence, for as I have told you, he was a quarrelsome sort of a man. But he had no drink in him today, and he just stood there gaping stupidly at the Factor. He could speak no English, but he understood it a little, though maybe not enough to make out the sense of Mr Sellar's words.

Hugh Macbeath stepped up to the Factor now, and asked him civilly would he permit his old bedridden father to remain, explaining that indeed he could not walk at all, and had a great sore on his eye.

'You must all be gone by Tuesday at the latest,' says Sellar, raising his voice. 'Well or ill. Deil a one shall remain.'

'That's a terrible thing whatever,' sighed Macbeath.

'It is no business of yours,' snapped the Factor. And then he called his head-shepherd to him, and wrote something down in his pocket-book, I suppose it was Hugh Macbeath's name.

My father propounded questions to us out of the Shorter Catechism as he always did that evening; but though I had done well at the examination by the Presbytery this year, I was not able to answer my father when he asked me to explain the doctrine of Election. I could not get out of my mind the look and the voice of Patrick Sellar, and in such a mood I was that truly I wondered was he the Son of Cursing who had taken human shape.

My father had planned for us to leave early on the Monday, for there would be much to do, you may imagine, making some sort of temporary shelter for ourselves in the desolate, uninhabited place which was to be our new home. But our leaving was delayed because of the poor natural, Cailein Bochd.

He was like one of those phantom beings we called the Glaistig. Ach, you will not have heard of them maybe, boy, for such old superstitions have died out among us in this new land. A Glaistig was supposed to be some former mistress of a house, who had been put under enchantments, a harmless creature who haunted her old habitation, and for whom a little milk was left out in the byre every evening. Harmless enough indeed was Cailein Bochd, and like the Glaistig he was attached not so much to people but to the house where he chose to stay.

Ever since my father had begun to dismantle our home, the natural had grown very agitated. My mother had tried to explain to him, in the sign-language she had invented, why we must be gone, but he had only neighed at her, staring with his poor vacant eyes and waving his great long ungainly arms. Now today when he saw us load the shelties with our belongings, and my mother take down the great iron pot and put out the fire, Cailein Bochd crouched down beside the cold hearth and snarled at us, like some beast daring us to touch him; and though we tried all we knew to persuade him to come with us, he would not do it at all.

'We must leave him,' said my mother at last. 'Not even this man of little soul, Patrick Sellar, would be harming a poor natural.'

When we had tramped the ten miles to Aird-an-Casgaich, there was so much to do, what with building a rude bothy to shelter us from the weather before we could start upon a proper house, and attending to our livestock, that the thought of the natural went out of my mind. But when she was bidding me good-night, my mother said to me:

'Donald, I am very much troubled in myself concerning Cailein Bochd. I thought that by now he would have followed us, and fear is on me that if there is any violence tomorrow in Strath Naver, what wits he has left will be altogether taken from him.'

I told her eagerly that I would return to Rossal early next morning and make another attempt to persuade the natural to come to us. And so it was, Donald Og, that I witnessed what was done in Strath Naver on that black Tuesday, June 13th.

I was up before the sun rose, and off on my walk. Dear heart! Never had the strath looked so beautiful as it did that day. There had been much snow in April, so that my dear Mountain of the Maiden resembled the head of some venerable bard, lifting itself above the rich firs that mantled it, its purity making drab the background of heaven. It occupied the sky like a throne, that mountain that had always seemed to me like a bastion protecting us from the alien world of the South; every granite pleat was distinct and separate upon it, its smocked breast the colour of a rose, and the shadows in the gullies slate-blue.

And how peaceful and lovely was the strath! The rocks beside the track along which I hurried were inlaid with dazzling quartz and embroidered with emerald mosses, and a little breeze stirred the forest of heather on the slopes, as though it rang a million tiny bells. When I saw all the small round houses, snug as bee-skeps, in that well populated strath, and the homely peat-reek going up straight and blue from each, I felt it was some evil dream my father had suffered to make him tear up his roots and forsake the earth on which his fathers had dwelt from time beyond counting.

Our folk were busy as usual, leading out the sheep to be tethered in the haughs, cutting the hay, milking the cows, weeding the ridges of arable where already there showed the tender green shoots of corn. A party of girls sat, arms linked, upon the ground, vigorously fulling cloth with their bare feet, swaying their shoulders in time to the spirited air they were singing, a melody echoed by a woman going to herd cattle.

And yet, and yet, Donald Og, the face and the voice of Patrick Sellar were still in my mind, and I knew that the crisis was at hand, that evil was in the very perfumed air of summer, and that the Namhairich were doomed.

I got greetings in all the townlands I passed, mixed up with some sharp jests on my father's being so ready to flit, ay, and reproaches for his lack of trust in God. It was terrible to me how, even after the Minister's sermon last Sabbath, and Sellar's words in the churchyard, they would not believe that the hour had struck; it was as though a spell had been cast upon them, as in a fairy-tale.

I had just reached Rossal, our own clachan, when a shout brought all the folk to their doors; and there, marching along the drove-road like a troop of soldiers, came some twenty men.

Have you ever observed, my son, the strange fearful silence that falls on little creatures when a hawk is sighted? So it was now with the folk of Rossal. I tell you, the very cattle stopped grazing and dogs forbore to bark, as Sellar on his pony, with his mob of Sheriff's officers and underlings, came into Rossal on that fair summer morning. The batons of the officers, and the picks and levers shouldered by the rest, told us all too plainly on what business they were bent. They halted at a sign from the Factor, and one among them read aloud a warrant; though I understood the English very well, I could scarcely make out a word of it, for it was all in some strange legal gibberish.

Now as I have told you, the house of William Chisholm stood apart from the other townlands, beside a burn which he used for his distilling. It was the first house in the path of the invaders; I knew that Chisholm would be up at his hidden still on the hillside, and it was his wife I had seen just now away to herd her cows. It flashed through my mind that the aged woman, his mother-in-law, would be alone in the house, and as I saw the officers begin to pull off the thatch and stick their picks into the walls, I ran thither as hard as I could, shouting:

'There is a woman near a hundred years of age in-by, who cannot stir from her bed.'

Sellar turned at my voice; and oh my grief! the face of him! I tell you it was the face of the Evil One himself, not ferocious, not threatening, but with a cold smile upon it as though he were at work he enjoyed. He stooped, and called through the low doorway, cheerily as one who made a joke:

'Get up, old hag, or you will have a hot bed!'

'She cannot do it at all,' I insisted, tugging at his coat. 'There is no power in her limbs to rise.'

'Is that so?' said he. 'She'll dance before I've finished with her.'

He turned to his men and gave them orders, still with that ghastly gaiety:

'Bring here some fir branches, kick away the peats on the hearth and light me some torches. Then strip off the outer layer from the thatch; fern is a cunning protection, and you'll find good kindling underneath.'

For some moments I stood petrified with horror, watching as in a daze as the men lit their torches from their victim's own hearthstone, tore away the fern thatching, and applied their burning brands to the highly inflammable bog-pine battens under it. Soon there arose a tongue of flame, livid in the sunlight; it ran along the roof as swift as a rat, spitting at bits of fern upon its journey, burrowing down into the rafters, gathering strength and hungering the more as it devoured. Then one of the men cried suddenly to Sellar:

'It is the truth, sir; there's an ancient woman within.'

'She has lived too long,' said this devil. 'Let her burn!'

Chisholm had now come bounding down the hillside, and the sight of him bringing me back to myself, we both of us dived into the burning house. Mistress Mackay was there in the box-bed from which she had never stirred for fourteen years, and as I had so often seen her do before, she was scrabbling with her skeleton hands at a certain crevice in the wall.

'The three pounds for my funeral!' she was muttering. 'Hoarded since I was wed.'

So that was the mysterious treasure about which we had so often speculated. But there was no time to try to rescue her savings; her blankets were afire, and we must get her out. Ochon, never shall I forget how she moaned at us:

'What fire is this about me? God receive my soul!'

We beat out the flames with our bare hands, and carried her up to Chisholm's bothy on the hill, where she became insensible, and not another word ever passed her lips.

When this was done, Chisholm became like a madman. By this time the battens and the walls of his house had fallen in, and the blaze from them had caught his growing corn, equal in extent to what would have brought twelve sheaves in harvest. He rolled upon the flames, flaying with his arms hither and thither as though he cared not whether he burnt himself to death if only he could save his little crop. And what was most terrible of all was to see Sellar fling down on the ground beside him three shillings, in compensation for the bog-fir that was perishing with the upland timber, and to hear that evil one say with a laugh:

'There's a fine bonfire for you! That will smoke the vermin out right enough. Hey, lads, it's hot work, but you shall have a dram to wet your whistle afterwards.'

I think they must have tasted a dram or two before they started, those men, for some of them were ordinary decent folk, and would never have been induced to take part in such frightfulness without the whisky in them. Indeed I saw one of them, Andrew Ross, the official appraiser of the estate, covertly give Chisholm three shillings more for the bog-fir out of pity. But though they were, I am sure, reluctant at the start of it, now they became evilly excited, seeming to find relief only in the bustle of devastation, seized with the mania of a mob who wantonly destroy.

When they had done with Chisholm, the Factor barked out a command, and away they went into the clachan, with me at their heels. I had been certain that the burning would be confined to Chisholm's house, remembering how Sellar had threatened him last Sabbath; but not at all. From house to house they went with their torches, the lust for wholesale destruction growing in them, so that a shepherd who was with them deliberately set on his collies to harry our live-stock, and the rest were flinging furniture down the brae.

My sorrow! If you could have seen the pitiful efforts of the Namhairich to save their little treasures! Pots and pans, presses, clothing, meal-kists, cheeses, away they all went tumbling down towards the river, and after them with lamentations and screaming our folk stumbled to rescue what they could. Here I saw a woman with an armful of fowls, their feathers all singed from the fire, there another scrabbled among the ruins for her distaff, or a silver bodkin, or the sett of tartan handed down through generations. The terrified lowing of the cattle-beasts was pitiful to hear, and even though it was aflame the menfolk would be carrying away their bog-fir where they could get it.

Down came Hugh Macbeath's house, except for one small portion of it where his sick old father lay, and that unroofed. Apart from this, which the sheriff's officers in their humanity let stand, no dwelling was spared; only a few huts containing the paupers on the parish-roll were left standing, and I heard Sellar threaten these poor folk that if they gave shelter to any of the evicted even for a moment, they also would be turned adrift. And besides the houses, he caused our common kiln to be destroyed, ay, and our barns, though by the custom of the country the out-going tenants had the use of these until they had manufactured their waygoing crops.

Many a tale could I tell of what I saw on that terrible day. But there is one memory that would remain with me though all the rest faded. It is of Cailein Bochd.

So distraught was I that half the work of destruction was

over in Rossal before I recalled the errand that had brought me back to the clachan that morning. I ran, then, to the skeleton of my old home, and there I found the natural, still squatting on the ground beside the cold hearthstone as though he had never moved since the previous day; he was gibbering to himself, and clutching to his breast a bunch of alder-wands with which he was used to fashion his little wicker carts. I shouted to him, through the roar and crackle of the flames, to come away, forgetting that he only understood my mother's sign-language. So then I put my arms about him, and strove to drag him outside.

But Cailein Bochd possessed in good measure the perverse obstinacy of his kind. This, though dismantled, was still his home, and like a stubborn child he dug his heels in, holding fast with his hands to the skeleton of our house, and such strength there was in him that I could no more have moved one of the great boulders by the river. While I was still wrestling with him, there came figures looming through the smoke, and I heard Sellar's voice ask angrily why this house was still unfired. Mastering my own anger, I ran to the Factor, shouting to him that my father had flitted peaceably the day before, leaving the upland timber of his house behind him.

'And an inhabitant besides,' sneered the Factor. 'Turn that drooling idiot away, my lads.'

His men approached Cailein Bochd, who still squatted there on the floor, and I think he must have thought them demons, for so they now appeared, with the sweat running down their blackened faces and their clothes in wild disorder, and their picks and axes menacing. Cailein Bochd let out a bellow like some wounded beast, as these men laid hold on him, flaying about him with his ape-like arms, so that they in their turn became terrified, and their terror made them the more brutal. Four of them were not enough to overpower him, such unnatural strength had he; but then one came behind him with a torch, thrusting it against his unkempt hair.

Oh God! I was minded of the man in the Gospel story, whose name was Legion and who dwelt in the tombs. As though they had been but children, Cailein Bochd flung off his captors as easily as Legion broke his chains, and giving again that fearful animal screech, he fled into the hills, a living torch. Never was he seen again, and it is my wound to think what did become of the poor creature.

I was with the trail of homeless who struggled along the track into exile at the close of that day. Few able-bodied young men there were amongst us, for most of these were away in strange lands fighting for Herself and their country, or else they were up in the shieling-huts. There were plenty tottering old men and women, there were wives heavy with child, or else dragging their little ones after them, crying with terror, and there were the sick. Ay, it was against such defenceless folk as these that Mr Patrick Sellar would make war!

Behind us, rolling through the strath like an infernal banner, came a column of smoke, thick, acrid, and shot with flame, and down in its bed the Naver seemed like a stream of dark blood from the reflection of the glare. We were as our first parents when they were turned out of Eden, but we through no fault of our own. I heard the voices of the eagles sailing down from their eyries in the Mountain of the Maiden, screaming for the feast of the charred corpses of the sheep and poultry we had not been able to save.

And in my heart also there was kindled a fire. Boy though I was, I vowed, Donald Og, that I would make this outrage known to all the world, that I would never rest until I had brought it home to the ravishers of my people, dedicating my life to that one purpose.

7

PRIVATE DIARY OF ELIZABETH, COUNTESS OF SUTHERLAND, 1815

April 23rd. We returned to Stafford House from Windsor this morning, somewhat fatigued by the celebrations of St George's Day, though these were more subdued than usual in consequence of the news of Napoleon's escape from Elba.

Amongst the pile of correspondence which awaited me, there was a letter from Mr Robert Mackid, Sheriff-Depute of Sutherlandshire, which letter has thrown me into great disturbance of mind. It seems that the tenants who were removed from Strath Naver last June collected among themselves a sum of money wherewith they have employed Mr Henderson, a man of business in Caithness, for the purpose of drawing up a Memorial to me. (Surely this proves that they cannot be so destitute as certain rumours would make them out to be?) The said Memorial Mr Mackid enclosed in his letter, and I read it before his own communication, growing more indignant with every word, for I am sure it is a pack of lies.

The tenants maintain that in consequence of the evictions, a woman near a hundred years of age, and a bedridden old man, have died. Besides these fatalities, they assert that the wife of John Mackay of Rhinovie (what dim memories of childhood such place-names recall!), insisting upon taking down the roof of her house herself, rather than permit the Sheriff's officers to do it, fell through the rafters and suffered a miscarriage. Further they allege that my Factor, Mr Sellar, illegally fired both their houses and barns. This I feel certain is untrue, for he is a man of law, and would be exact in observing it.

But when I turned to the letter of Mackid, my indignation gave place to acute uneasiness. He writes that a complaint having been made to him by the said Mr Henderson, he laid it before the Sheriff-Substitute. This Mr Cranstoun ordered him to take a precognition of the case, and, if there appeared sufficient cause, to arrest Patrick Sellar. In pursuance of this order, Mr Mackid has been to Sutherland, and personally has examined some forty witnesses from among the tenants who were removed. His letter is that of a man very deeply shocked, and he begs my permission to demand Sellar's resignation, and to offer some compensation to a multitude of poor persons who, he asserts, have been most grievously wronged.

'It is with the deepest regret,' he writes, 'that I have to inform your ladyship that a more numerous catalogue of crimes, perpetrated by an individual, has seldom disgraced any country, or sullied the pages of a precognition in Scotland.'

I am at a loss to know what I should do. The descriptions given me by Mr Mackid (who must be a gentleman of probity, seeing the office he holds) of the manner of the removals, and of the extreme misery and distress among the evicted, who have lost nearly all their last year's crop by the new tenant's cattle having got at it, touches a sympathetic cord in my bosom. On the other hand, I feel sure that what he writes must be exaggerated; no lawyer would have dared to act in the way Sellar is said to have done, setting aside the fact that no man of common humanity would behave so.

One of the witnesses examined by Mr Mackid was named William Macleod, and someone of that name used to bring me every year a hamper of gifts, butter, cheese, venison, and the like, from my tenants when I was a child at my grand-mother's house in Edinburgh. But I must not be foolish; that has nothing whatever to do with the present case, and besides, William Macleod is a very common name in Sutherland.

March 30th. Having pondered much upon the tenants' Memorial and Mr Mackid's letter, I took the opportunity of laying them both before George when we were drinking tea after dinner this evening, there being no guests. He was vexed at being troubled with what he termed so trifling a matter when the whole of Europe is under threat of another war, not to speak of the conflict in which our arms are engaged in North America. It was infernal impudence, he asserted, in these peasants to address me.

'But I am their Chief, George,' I reminded him. 'I cannot but be touched by their stubborn belief in my care for their welfare, a belief they have retained though all my life I have been absent from them.'

'You are their landlord, my dear,' replied George firmly. 'You really must try not to be so sentimental.'

'But this man Sellar,' I insisted. 'I know nothing of him personally. Pray tell me your opinion of his character.'

'He is a civilised person and a lawyer,' said my husband. 'Moreover, he holds office under the Crown. Do you think it likely that such a man would have committed the enormities attributed to him by these ignorant peasants?'

Dear George! so sane and realistic. I lean on him more and more as I grow older. He dictated to me a reply I must send to Mr Mackid, and though privately I deem it very cold, I must bow to my husband's superior wisdom. He bade me write in the third person thus:

'The Countess of Sutherland thanks you for your communication, and for the enclosure which she returns herewith. If any person on her estate shall receive any illegal treatment, she will never consider it as hostile to her if they have recourse to legal redress, as the most secure way to receive the justice which she always desires they should have upon every occasion.'

June 20th. In the midst of the celebrations for our most glorious victory at Waterloo, I was dismayed to receive another letter from Mr Mackid, informing me that, the Sheriff-Substitute being strongly of the opinion that illegal acts have been committed by my Factor, he ordered Mr Mackid to arrest Mr Sellar, which he did on May 31st. That he has struck Mr Sellar from the roll of procurators practising before his court, has imprisoned him in Dornoch jail, forwarding to the Lord Advocate of Scotland the testimony taken by Mackid from the late tenants of Strath Naver, and finally, that the Lord Advocate has ordered a public trial.

Scarcely ventured to mention this communication to George. At such a time of national rejoicing, the affairs of my Scottish estate seem petty indeed! Introduced the subject by commenting upon the gallant part played by the Black Watch, the Gordons, and other Highland regiments at Waterloo, but George not at all impressed.

'No one has ever denied your countrymen's appetite for fighting,' said he, 'which they share with other barbarians.'

He went on to remark, with some irritation, that this business of Sellar's arrest could not have come at a more inopportune moment for him—I mean for my husband.

'The old King cannot last much longer,' said he, 'and I look for a dukedom when Prinney gets the throne. He forsook the Whigs when he was made Prince Regent, but he will need our pursestrings opened for him then. You do not suppose that I have paid his gambling debts more than once without expectation of some just reward? And then there is this marriage I am arranging for Elizabeth with Lord Blantyre; we cannot afford the least breath of scandal, and I shall have to use my influence to ensure that your Factor does not come up for trial. It is the sort of thing which would hugely delight our agitators, with their constant cry of the oppression of the poor by the rich.'

Cancelled my engagement at the opera, and spent the evening with my sewing-woman, making garments for our poor West Indian slaves.

8

YESTERDAY there was held at the Circuit Court of
Justiciary in this town a very notable trial, to wit, that of
Mr Patrick Sellar, Factor to the most noble the Marchioness
of Stafford and Countess of Sutherland.

Our readers may remember that it is now nearly a year
since this unfortunate gentleman was arrested, during all
which time he has languished in Dornoch jail. Meanwhile
the public mind has been agitated by the most mischievous
rumours in certain newspapers (which at no time have
circulated among the educated classes in Scotland), to the
effect that Mr Sellar was guilty of extreme cruelty in the
removal of the small tenants from the tract called Strath
Naver, in the County of Sutherland, in the summer of 1814.

Immense interest, therefore, was excited by the news that
Mr Sellar was at last to have an opportunity of clearing
himself from these charges, for it was felt by many that every
Highland proprietor, sheep-farmer, and factor was involved
in his case. The Circuit Court was packed almost to suffoca-
tion, and those of our readers who were not able to gain
admittance on this historic occasion will, we are confident,
appreciate some account of the proceedings.

The learned Judge, the Hon. David Monypenny of
Pitmilly, one of the Lords Commissioners of Justiciary,
having taken his seat, the fifteen jurymen already named by
him were sworn. They were all, our readers will be gratified
to hear, most respectable persons, being either merchants,

small landed proprietors, sheep-farmers or ground-officers. The indictment was of great length, and we must content ourselves with giving our readers a condensation of it.

The pannel was indicted and accused at the instance of Archibald Colquhon of Killermont, His Majesty's Advocate for His Majesty's interest, of culpable homicide, as likewise of oppression and real injury, more particularly, 'the wickedly and maliciously setting on fire and burning a great extent of heath and pasture, on which a number of small tenants maintained their cattle; the violently turning or procuring to be turned out of their habitations a number of the said tenants, especially aged and infirm and impotent persons, and pregnant women, and cruelly depriving them of all cover and shelter, to their great distress and the imminent danger of their lives; the demolishing of kilns, barns, dwelling houses, mills, growing corn, timber, furniture and other effects, the lawful possessions of the said tenants'.

'And true it is,' concluded the indictment, 'and of verity, that you the said Patrick Sellar, are guilty of the said heinous crimes, or of one or more of them, actor or art and part.'

Mr Sellar having pleaded Not Guilty, one of his counsel, Mr Cockburn, read two objections, the first being concerned with the relevancy of the libel, and the second with its truth.

'The pannel will prove,' continued Mr Cockburn, 'that the ejections which have given rise to this trial were done in due order of law, and under the warrants of the proper Judge, issued on regular process. Further he will prove that great indulgence was shown to the tenants even after they had resisted the regular decrees of the Judge; that nothing was done on his part, or with his knowledge or approval, either cruel, oppressive or illegal; and, on the whole he will prove, that throughout every part of this affair he has been the victim not only of the most unfounded local prejudices but of long continued and active defamation on the part of certain persons—'(and here our reporter observed counsel to look very pointedly at Mr Mackid, the Sheriff-Depute) '—who made it their business to traduce the whole system of improvements introduced into the Sutherland Estate, and to vilify the pannel, by whom they have been pleased to suppose that these improvements have been partly conducted.'

Mr Cockburn concluded his objections with the remark that the pannel rejoiced at the first opportunity which had been afforded him of meeting these calumnies in a Court of Justice, and that, relying as he did on the candour and dispassionate attention of a British Jury, he had no doubt whatever of being able to establish his complete innocence of all the charges brought against him.

Our reporter was indeed impressed by the confident demeanour of Mr Sellar throughout the proceedings, an air in marked contrast to that of certain underlings who were named in the indictment as those who had assisted him in the removals.

Mr Patrick Robertson, advocate, opened the case for the defence. Having objected to those parts of the indictment which contained general charges, as, 'destroying a number of houses', 'firing a number of barns', etc., he gave a most concise sketch of the causes which had led to this trial, as the clamour in the country, the prejudice of ignorant peasants, the disgraceful publications in certain vulgar newspapers, notably *The Military Register* which, unhappily, circulates among all ranks of our armed forces, and the pains taken to introduce these false and mischievous papers throughout the Highlands. There was even a rumour, said he, to the effect that the lapse of time between Mr Sellar's arrest and his being brought to trial, had been due to the influence of the most noble the Marquis and Marchioness of Stafford, who had hoped to avoid a public examination of their Factor. To such lengths will prejudice go!

Mr Robertson then stated his general line of defence. As for the heath burning, it had been done at the express consent of the tenantry, and to their positive advantage, since it cleaned the ground. For the removings, Mr Sellar had been preferred as the highest bidder at the set at Golspie, when the lands in question had been auctioned at the New Inn there; he had brought regular decrees and precepts of ejection, which were now in the hands of the Clerk of the Court. For the demolition of houses and barns, none had been pulled down until the ejections were completed, and the property had become the pannel's. No furniture had been destroyed by himself or by his orders, no unnecessary violence had been used, nor any cruelty exercised, but everything had been carried out in due order of law.

'The charges of culpable homicide,' concluded Mr Robertson, 'are quite out of the question, and the pannel defies the Public Prosecutor to prove them. Upon the whole, it is not doubted that if truth and justice are to prevail over malice and conspiracy, Mr Sellar will obtain an honourable and triumphant acquittal.'

The Advocate-Depute here stated that he did not mean to insist on any charges except those which were specifically mentioned in the indictment. Before the Crown called its witnesses, the learned Judge made the following remarks:

'It would be improper for me to enter at present into the origin of the prosecution, or the nature of the defence. Neither shall I say anything of the publications which have been alluded to, except that they appear to be of the most contemptible nature, and the only prejudice I can ascertain is the other way; that is, against the cause requiring such aid. I have no doubt of the relevancy of the libel.'

There here occurred a most disgraceful incident. A person among the spectators, by his dress a half-pay officer, said loudly that *The Military Register* was the journal of those who had served their country to the admiration of all in the Peninsular and on other battlefields. That Britain was only too eager to appeal to the Highlanders to fight her wars for her, making false promises of bounty and protection in return.

The crush being so great, and this person being at the very back of the Court Room, the ushers were not able to eject him before he had read aloud a letter from the Colonel of one, William Macleod, of the 93rd Regiment, who had been killed in the desperate but unsuccessful attack on the Mississippi in 1814. This letter was to the effect that the said Macleod, though wounded in both legs, had propped himself against a bank and continued to play his comrades on upon the bagpipes until he was shot dead. 'His bearing has added lustre to the name of his regiment and of his country.'

'In reward for which valour,' shouted this offensive person, 'his father and kinsfolk have been outed from their land.'

This unseemly interruption might have had the most dangerous consequences, for a section of the spectators so far forgot themselves as to raise a cheer. But a threat from the learned Judge that he would clear the Court if there was any more of such disgraceful behaviour had its due effect, and, the original interrupter having been ejected, the trial continued.

The interest of the proceedings was considerably enhanced at this point when a number of witnesses, persons who had been removed from their dwellings in Strath Naver, were called by the Crown. Many having no English, their testimony was translated by Mr Ross, Sheriff-Substitute of the County of Ross-shire. Eleven in all gave their testimony, which appeared to our reporter in the highest degree exaggerated and unlikely.

In particular one, William Chisholm, a most disreputable-looking ruffian, insisted that Mr Sellar had set fire to his house while his aged mother-in-law was within, and that being apprised of her presence, the pannel had exclaimed, 'She has lived too long; let her burn!' There was some excusable laughter when, Chisholm having sworn that this ancient dame had died the following Sunday from exposure, it was ascertained that she was no less than a hundred years of age. As Mr Robertson wittily enquired, did her son-in-law imagine her to be immortal?

A somewhat similar charge was brought by Hugh

Macbeath, who swore that his house had been destroyed while his sick old father was within it, and that in consequence the said father had died ten days later. It transpired under cross-examination, however, that in fact that portion of the house in which the old man lay was spared. After these eleven witnesses had been examined, the Crown would have called others, having, as they said, a vast number in attendance, but the defence successfully objected, in respect that they were erroneously described in the list served on the pannel.

We must enlighten our readers, who cannot be expected to have much acquaintance with these wild tribes, and their strange customs, that it is their habit to give themselves several names. Claiming as they do descent from a common ancestor, all take his name, as for example Sutherland, and a second to designate the particular branch from which they come, which last is the genealogical surname, or *bun sloine*. But as if this were not enough, they must give each other nicknames, as Peter-with-the-beard, John-blind-in-one-eye, Ewen-the-strong, and other ridiculous appellations.

The Crown urged with seriousness that this nicknaming was strictly necessary, instancing the fact that there were no less than seventeen William Mackays in Captain Sackville's company in the 93rd, and more than a hundred of that ilk in the whole regiment. But the learned Judge here interposed with the ruling that, however that might be, in law the witnesses were erroneously named, and moreover that at this late hour it would be quite superfluous to occupy the time of the Court with any more such testimony.

The Rev. David Mackenzie then identified the notice given to the tenants at the set at Golspie, a notice he had interpreted to them in their native tongue on that occasion. He stated further that some weeks afterwards, Mr Sellar observing to him that the tenants were dilatory in removing, the reverend gentleman replied that, there being no allotments ready for them, it was impossible for them to remove.

William Young Esq., Commissioner to the noble proprietors on their Sutherland estate, was called to explain the reason for this. He informed the Court that his intention had been to have the allotments ready for them in the spring, and that a land surveyor had arrived in April to examine the ground. Unfortunately he had scarcely set foot in Sutherlandshire when news came that his wife was taken sick, and he was forced to return home. However, said Mr Young, the marking off of the allotments had been completed by June 4th. The houses there, he added, were to be built by the tenants, but meantime there were some old barns in which they could have taken shelter, at least as good as the wretched hovels they formerly inhabited.

After some other formalities, with which we will not burthen our readers, the Advocate-Depute declared that the proof for the prosecution was concluded.

It was stated on the part of the pannel that he had intended to have adduced as witnesses to his character, Sir George Abercrombie of Birkenbog, Bart., Sheriff-Depute of Elgin and Nairn, George Fenton Esq., Sheriff-Substitute of the same, and James Brodie Esq., of Brodie; but by a most unlucky coincidence all these gentlemen had been visited by sickness at the same time. It was proposed by the defence to read letters from them containing their opinion of Mr Sellar's character, although counsel admitted that this was not regular evidence.

The Advocate-Depute making no objection, however, the letters were read. They were almost identical in wording, and spoke of Mr Sellar as being 'a man of sympathy and feeling', 'of the strictest integrity and humanity', 'incapable of being even an accessory to any cruel or oppressive action'. Thomas Gilzean Esq., Sheriff-Substitute for the County of Inverness, and Sir Archibald Dunbar, Bart., were in Court and spoke to the same purpose.

Witnesses were then called who had been present at, or had assisted in, the removals, eminently respectable persons, as John Dryden, head-shepherd, John Burns, farmer, Andrew Ross, official appraiser, Duncan Ross, ground-officer, and several others. All agreed that everything had been done in the gentlest manner, that all the moss-fir had been strictly paid for, that nothing had been destroyed until the warrants were read and all the furniture and other effects removed, and that all sick persons had been allowed to remain. In particular, great care had been taken to leave standing a sufficient portion of Hugh Macbeath's house to accommodate his father who was old and infirm.

One witness, James Fraser, used the unfortunate expression, 'There was no unnecessary cruelty', for which he was sharply rebuked by the learned Judge.

Mr Home-Drummond spoke briefly for the prosecution. The Crown, he said, now gave up all charges except those which concerned the destruction of barns, and of real injury done to the ancient woman, Margaret Mackay. He certainly did not think that the evidence in her case was sufficient to establish culpable homicide; but he argued that the circumstances proved were enough to authorise the jury in finding a verdict of guilty to the extent of injury, as she had been removed at the risk of her life, which he maintained was contrary to law. In regard to the barns, he contended that the conduct of the pannel was irregular, and consequently oppressive, the out-going tenants being entitled 'by the custom of the country' to retain these barns as long as the arable land.

Mr Gordon for the defence spoke at much greater length, going deeply into the history and object of the prosecution. It was, he asserted, a preconceived plan in which certain persons had instigated the ignorant peasants of Strath Naver to complain at first, and to persist afterwards. He spoke eloquently of the views these persons entertained of successfully opposing the improvements in Sutherlandshire, and arresting the progress of civilisation through the sides of Mr Sellar; and of the disgraceful measures to which these persons had resorted with a view to obstruct the channels of justice, the impartiality of jurymen, and the purity of evidence. He attacked the conduct of Mr Mackid in the most pointed terms; exposed the character of the Crown witnesses, in particular that of William Chisholm, a vicious person who lived by illicit distilling; and dwelt on the clear evidence of the total innocence of Mr Sellar with so much feeling that our reporter has confessed he felt the tears come into his eyes.

Mr Gordon concluded thus:

'I maintain that this is not merely the trial of Patrick Sellar, but in truth a conflict between the law of the land and resistance to that law, between order and anarchy, between progress and reaction. That the question at issue involves the future fate of agricultural, ay, and even of moral improvements in the County of Sutherland and throughout the Highlands; that (though certainly not intended by the Public Prosecutor, whose conduct has been candid, correct and liberal) it is, nevertheless, in substance and in fact, a trial of strength between the abettors of misrule and the magistracy, as well as the laws, of Great Britain.'

It was plain to our reporter that the manly bosoms of the jury were moved by this eloquent oration.

The learned Judge summed up with that strict impartiality which is the glory of our legal system. It was unnecessary, he said, for the jury to consider any of the charges except the destruction of barns and that concerning the old woman, Margaret Mackay. As to the first, there could be no doubt of the old practice of the country of retaining these barns until the crops were reaped and threshed. Neither could it be doubted that the pannel had not left the whole of the barns for the use of the out-going tenants, and in consequence of this they had suffered damage.

But, continued his lordship emphatically, in point of law the pannel was not bound by any such practice, but was entitled to proceed, as the in-coming tenant, to do what he wished with his own. In regard to the injury said to be done to Margaret Mackay, witnesses for the pannel contradicted those for the Crown, and it was the duty of the jury to decide between them.

'If you are at a loss,' said his lordship, 'I must remind you that you ought to take into view the character of the accused, for this is always of importance in balancing contradictory testimony. Now, in the first place there has been a host of witnesses who have testified to Mr Sellar's humanity of disposition; it is true that some of this testimony, being from persons absent, is not strictly evidence; nevertheless, the eminence of these persons, several of whom are officers of the Crown, must have some weight with you. And in the second place there are the actual eye-witnesses of the removals, of humble station it is true, but not to be despised on that account. All of these have sworn that Mr Sellar's conduct was most humane and honourable.

'Pray, now,' concluded his lordship, 'go and converse among yourselves in another room.'

The jury returned after a very brief interval with a unanimous verdict of 'Not Guilty,' which somewhat surprised certain among the spectators who, it seems, had expected a 'Not Proven'. The learned Judge told the jury that his opinion concurred completely with theirs, and that in dismissing them after so long a trial he was happy to say they had paid the most patient attention to the case, and had returned a verdict satisfactory to the Court. He was then pleased to address Mr Sellar in the following gracious terms:

'Mr Sellar, it is now my duty to dismiss you from the bar; and you have the satisfaction of thinking that you are discharged by the unanimous opinion of the jury and the Court. I am sure that, though your feelings must have been agitated, you cannot regret that this trial took place; and I am hopeful that it will have due effect upon the minds of the country, which have been so much and so improperly disturbed.'

The Court then pronounced an interlocutor, in respect of the verdict of the assize, assoiling the pannel *simpliciter*; and so ended this most notable trial.

9

LETTER FROM PATRICK SELLAR
TO JAMES LOCH

BURGHEAD, Morayshire, North Britain. May 4th, 1817.

Pray accept, my dear Sir, my most hearty felicitations upon your appointment as Commissioner for the Marquis and Marchioness of Stafford's Sutherland Estate. That you must combine these new duties with the onerous task of administering his lordship's properties in England must needs place a heavy burthen on your shoulders. Nevertheless, I cannot but rejoice that you accepted the appointment after the resignation of Mr Young.

Far be it from me to say a word in disparagement of this gentleman, who has always treated me fairly; only I cannot help deploring the timorous spirit which caused him to resign soon after the happy issue of my trial. To say, as he did, that the public were obviously dissatisfied with the verdict was an unworthy remark. To be moved by the vulgar outcry of the lower orders, who are permanently envious of what is of advantage to their betters, proves Mr Young to have been no fit person to carry on his responsibilities.

It has been justly remarked that Providence knows how to bring good out of evil; and it may be that but for the malice of certain persons in bringing me to trial, this estate would have been denied the management of so experienced and enlightened a gentleman as your good self.

I am not, I hope, a vindictive character, and had I no feelings to consult except my own, I should have rested satisfied with the resignation of Mr Cranstoun and Mr Mackid from the offices of Sheriff-Substitute and Sheriff-Depute respectively. But so blatant was the conspiracy and malice proved against Mr Mackid, so loud his expressions of sympathy with the sub-tenants, and of disapproval (to give it no stronger word) of the conduct of the noble proprietors, that I felt it my public duty to threaten him with a law-suit.

I am happy to inform you that he has sent me just now the most submissive, nay, the most abject apology, from which I quote:

'That you would be entitled to exemplary damages from me, for my participation in the injury done you, I am most sensible; and I shall, therefore, not only acknowledge it as a most important obligation conferred on me and my innocent family, if you will have the goodness to drop your law-suit against me, but I shall pay the expenses of that suit and place at your disposal towards the reimbursement of the previous expenses which this most unfortunate business has occasioned you, any sum you may exact. Only I beg that in naming it, you will take into account the state of my affairs, which are nearly bankrupt, I having been forced to resign my offices and to move into another county. I throw myself entirely on your generosity.'

I have demanded from Mr Mackid the very moderate sum of two hundred pounds, together with all my expenses.

I cannot omit to mention to you that, while the outed tenants of Strath Naver appear for the most part satisfied with their new allotments, one young lad among them is likely to prove a trouble-maker. This Donald Macleod is the brother of Piper William Macleod, mentioned at my trial by the former tacksman, Captain Gordon, who made such an unseemly interruption during the proceedings. The youth was one of the witnesses for the Crown who were not permitted to give their evidence, on account of their being erroneously described in the list served on me; and he was heard to say afterwards that, 'this was a very convenient trick to stop my mouth and that of others'.

I am the more concerned because this Donald is now

apprenticed to his father, a good sort of man, who pursues the trade of mason for considerable periods in the Lowlands, where the youth is sure to be encouraged in his discontentment by the agitators who infest our towns. Donald, it appears, both speaks and writes English with surprising fluency, and altogether is a young spark who might light a flame of insurrection.

I have ordered all my ground-officers to be exact in observing him, and in reporting to me any disaffected words or actions.

10

DONALD MACLEOD'S STORY
continued

I NEVER would have believed that a people could have suffered such a change in spirits and in character as that which fell upon the Namhairich after their eviction from Strath Naver.

We had always been poor, as I have told you, but never destitute, for we helped one another in our difficulties, and if bad seasons came along, or cattle-plague, we applied as a matter of course to our good tacksman for relief. But now we knew the difference between poverty and destitution right enough. In place of our fertile strath we must make do with moorland, where the soil was but a thin reddish gravel under a layer of moss, good for nothing. Our allotments were so small that we had enough to do to keep a few head of stock to feed ourselves, and seldom had any to sell at the market.

But oh my child! what was worse than the physical degradation was the moral. Gradually I came to know the full horror of the deed done on that June day in Strath Naver. The barbarity that had evicted us had forced us to partake of its own nature; our people, so highly civilised, so steeped in great traditions, so deeply imbued with respect for our ancient laws, were hurled back almost into a state of primitive savagery. The law of the jungle, the survival of the fittest, the weakest to the wall, these had usurped in an evil hour our famous loyalty to friends, our generosity to the unfortunate, our reverence for authority.

After the trial of Patrick Sellar, despair had the Namhairich in its grip. Every voice on our behalf had been silenced, every pen laid down, and we lay helpless at the feet of our oppressors, whose weapons were legal quibbles. We had become but useless lumber, to be got rid of at any price.

The conduct of the ministers during the clearance caused religion to lose its hold; and vices, hitherto almost unknown among us, made their appearance, drunkenness, adultery, cheating. You know that while we have only one word in our language, *gruaim*, to express gloom, we have a score of words to express joy and merriment, for we are by nature a merry people. But och! we now became as gloomy as though the sun had set on us for ever. Our folk seemed to have lost their taste for ancient songs and dances; there was no shinty after work was done, no wrestling and putting the stone. In the winter evenings, instead of a *ceilidh* they would meet to moan about their wrongs and their fears for the future.

And in the dark of the moon, the young men would be off to dare the dogs of the shepherds, and would come home with a fat mutton.

'Hunger has a long arm,' they would say, quoting a Gaelic proverb when their fathers rebuked them.

All through my childhood I had heard the tale of a discharged soldier, William Mackay, who had been executed for horse-stealing. That was the only capital conviction for theft occurring in Sutherland between 1747 and 1810, and so it was the subject of conversation about the fireside for generations. But now stealing, expecially of sheep, became so common that the sheep-farmers formed themselves into associations to suppress it; and what was more dreadful was to see our folk beginning to put locks and bolts upon their doors, a thing never before seen in all the Highlands.

I was much away from home at this time, accompanying my father on his work as a stone-mason; and when we returned to Aird-an-Casgaich in the November of 1818 we were astonished to find our folk rejoicing. For news had reached them that Patrick Sellar had resigned his office as Factor, his name having become odious throughout Scotland.

'Thanks be to God!' my father cried fervently. 'Now he is gone, he and his dirty sheepskin charters, all will be well.'

Folk actually had come to refer to Sellar as *am fear nach fhiach*, the Worthless One, which as you know is one of our names for Satan. Had he not, they said, the marks of the Devil about him? He went to and fro through the earth; he had a strange voice, neither English nor Scots, and some said it resembled the bleating of a goat, always regarded as an infernal creature. Ay, there were even a few old wives who swore that where he had been walking they had seen the marks of a cloven hoof.

Hitherto a sense of insecurity had made all of us reluctant to try any improvements on our new land, wondering might it also be taken away from us. But the news of Sellar's resignation came as the lifting of a cloud, and we began to drain the moorland and build dykes. To me the news had a special joy about it, for now it would be right for me to ask for Fiona Gordon's hand in marriage.

You must understand that it was the rule with us for no young man to marry until he had the means to provide a home for his wife and for his future children. Since the evictions, having no certainty of being permitted to remain on their present lands, or of inheriting their father's croft, some of our young men had taken to marrying when they pleased. But that would not do for me at all; my darling must have a home as worthy as I could make it, with no fear of having to flit as her father had done from Strath Naver.

For some years past I had scrimped and saved the wages my father paid me as his apprentice, for money was the thing a man needed now, we being no longer self-supporting, no, nor paying part of our rent in labour as in the old days; and I well remember how I would sit up at night reckoning what it would cost me to set up house. The house itself I could build with my own hands, but I must pay a carpenter to make for us a press, a table, and a box-bed. My dear must have a spinning-wheel, for she was not handy with the distaff, and this would cost five shillings. We could not do with less than four wooden dishes, three pots, and ten horn spoons; we must have a pair of tongs, a crook and chain for the fire, and some churns and cheese-presses. And what would the tailor charge me for the new suit I must wear on my wedding-day? Still, I believed that I could manage.

You do not remember your mother, Donald Og, when she was herself. She was taken out of herself, as we say, on that terrible night when you were but seven years old, and which I must describe in its proper place. Let me try to tell you of the girl I married.

She had a lovely courage, the highest sort of courage, for she was by nature as timid as a hind, and always, every day of her life, she must be conquering some fear. She was an only child, and had lost her mother very early, and (though it is not to send it after him) her father was a hard man. Thus it was, I think, that she had come to live largely in a world of dreams as an escape, and would listen eagerly to tales of the People of Peace or Still Folk, so called by us because it was said that they could sometimes be seen but scarcely ever heard. I suspected that Fiona had the two-sights, that dreaded gift among us; for she had been born at midnight, and it was believed that such babes grew up to see things which are not meant for mortal eyes.

At anyrate she had an air of mystery which made some of the folk shun her, saying that she was proud. Maybe only I, who loved her so dearly from the roots of my heart, suspected what a fight she fought with fear.

A great compassion she had for the weak and helpless, so that all the dumb beasts were devoted to her, and she could do anything with them. In the leanest season of the year when, in our new destitute condition, we were famished, it was the custom to draw a little blood from the living cow and mix it with oatmeal to make a cake. Folk would send for Fiona when this must be done, for the cows would let her take their blood as readily as they would bring down their milk when she sang to them; but my grief! how she shrank from the task, though no one guessed it.

I see her now, clear as I see you, carrying a famished beast too weak to walk, up to the hills when the weather opened. And when a cow lost her calf, I see Fiona making what we called a *tulachan*, a sort of wooden dummy covered with the dead one's hide, and this she would be rocking skilfully with her foot, so that it imitated a calf sucking, until the mother, deceived by that which was so like her dead offspring, would cease her mournful mooing.

What grace and beauty was there, what rhythm in every task to which Fiona put her hand! I see her on a baking-day with her sleeves tucked up to the armpits, her fingers seeming to caress the oatmeal. I see her coming back from the shieling-huts when the summer was ended, her arm about the neck of a beast, her sweet true voice singing the old air of *Colin's Cattle*, a garland of wild flowers on her head, so lovely that there would rise in my mind the words of our bard Ossian, when he described the fair Aganideca, 'Like a new moon from clouds on sea, beauty enrobed her in light'.

For some years past we had always managed, whenever I was home, to be working on the same rick, to reap beside each other on the same harvest rigs, and to walk home together from the Mission House. And now at last my dear dream was coming true, and Fiona would be exchanging the snood of the maiden for the curch of the wife.

Yet, if I had not had such happiness in my heart, there were some things that would have made me sad enough, ay, and angry. When I went to Mr Mackenzie to ask him to officiate at the wedding, he made all sorts of objections. I could not understand it at all, until at last he told me plainly that he had orders from the higher powers to discourage our folk from marrying; the Highlands were already over-populated. When, as was the custom, Fiona and I went round our friends for miles to invite them to the wedding, many a silent clachan did I come across, many a ruined bothy and cold hearth. The Highlands over-populated! Not by two-legged inhabitants any longer, I am telling you that.

There was shame on me to be expecting the customary

gifts from folk who were now so destitute; but in spite of the change that had fallen on us since the evictions, a wedding was still an occasion when people would give without stint. The matrons of the families we visited returned our calls, and brought with them as usual the presents which would serve for the bridal feast and would help us in our first days of housekeeping; and there was plenty food and drink laid out in the barn for all comers on the day when Fiona and I were wed.

As I look back upon it now, I know that the merriment of that sweet day had a shadow on it, that some of the old fun was missing, though there was the scattering of the bride-cake as of old, and a scrambling of the young folk to get the first bit, and Fiona and I hiding from each other before the ceremony, and all the other customs. Good Mr Sage was the minister I would have had to marry us, but after the evictions in Strath Naver he had become a prey to melancholy and had removed to Aberdeen; and here was Mr Mackenzie instead, looking as sour when he tied the knot as though marrying were a sort of crime. And before the ceremony, when our two processions went to church, and there was the traditional firing off of shot-guns in every clachan on our route, the sound had an ominous note in it.

But all this I realised only afterwards. The memory I keep, and will keep locked up in my heart until I join her, is of my bride in all her little finery, her mother's silver brooch with a crystal in the centre of it, a string of green transparent pebbles round her creamy throat, her snood as white as our Highland streams could make it, and a treasured heirloom, a bronze armlet, on her wrist. She walked that day as though she had wings under her gown, and could fly if she had chosen to use them; her eyes were as blue as a lochan under the summer sky, and her voice was as sweet as the breeze in the corn-rigs, when she made her vows to me.

The year 1818 it was; I was just the same age as the century, and my bride a year behind me. A few months of bliss we had together; and then that evil befell us which we had imagined gone for ever when Patrick Sellar resigned his place.

I I

EXCHANGE OF LETTERS BETWEEN COMMISSIONER JAMES LOCH, M.P., AND THE REVEREND DAVID MACKENZIE

COMMISSIONER'S OFFICE, 2, Charlotte Square, Edinburgh. February 14th, 1818.

You are probably aware that a considerable change is to be made in the settlement of the people of your parish, which is to be completed by Whitsunday, 1819, by removing the inhabitants of the upper and lower parts of the strath to the sea-coast, extending from the mouth of the Naver to Strathy and Armadale.

You will indicate to the people of your parish that these removals are intended for their advantage, that they may live more comfortably and have the bounties of the ocean added to their means of livelihood. You will assure them that the measure has been too well considered not to be fully acted upon, and too well arranged not to be carried into effect. Indeed, the lands they hold are already let to others from Whitsunday, 1819.

I not only give you leave to show this letter, but beg that you will make it as public as possible.

Farr Manse, Sutherlandshire. February 21st, 1818.

From what I know of the circumstances of the majority of those around me, since so many were sent down from the heights to clear Mr Sellar's farm, I do not perceive how the great addition, which is intended to be made to their number, can live comfortably as you anticipate.

The lands of the coast are not extensive, neither are they good; the surface of the ground is extremely rugged and incapable of improvement, there being no lime nor marl, and but a scanty supply of seaware for manure. The coast, as you know, is remarkably bold and rocky, landing-places few, and some of them far from safe. There is no traffic or industry, nor any opportunity of earning money by day labour.

With my knowledge of these circumstances, and because I am yet ignorant of anything to be done for the people, further than upwards of a thousand of them are to be added to the population on the coast, I beg leave to be excused from giving them any assurance of the change being made to their advantage. I decline this task. You will readily allow, Sir, that it is a serious matter to remove, at one term, in one parish, more than four hundred families, who are still struggling with the unavoidable difficulties in which they have been placed, viz. the low price of cattle, reduction in the profits of day labour, poor soil, and above all the failure of last year's crop.

I am willing you lay this letter before Lord and Lady Stafford.

Postscriptum. The above was written for me by Jamie Munro, our new dominie, a fine scholar, the Lord having chastened me sair with the rheumaticks, so that I canna write but with pain. Pray, Mr Loch, put in a word for these puir folk with her ladyship; aiblins ye'll get them some relief.

Commissioner's Office, 2 Charlotte Square, Edinburgh. March 12th, 1818.

I have the favour of yours to hand. I regret to have to remind one of your cloth that your duty is to inform the people of the forthcoming removals, not to express your opinion concerning them, since they have been arranged by the noble proprietrix who gave you the living of Farr.

Pressure of business connected with my Lord Marquis's affairs constrains me to indicate to you that this correspondence is now closed.

12

DONALD MACLEOD'S STORY
continued

I HAD been but a short time married when I must tear myself away from the arms of my wife to go about my work, being now a master mason.

All through these years there had been grand new roads cut into our Sutherland, entirely for the convenience of the sheep-farmers, who, if you please, were exempted from the poll-tax called road-money, of four shillings on every male of eighteen years and upwards. You ask how it could have been so? I can answer only that Sutherland was a law unto itself, none daring to question this or other injustices. Just lately there had been a new road started, a twelve-foot gravelled carriage-way of forty-nine miles between Bonar Bridge and Tongue, costing no less than six hundred and fifty pounds for every mile of it. On this road I had got work, and I did not return to Aird-an-Casgaich until March, 1819.

The little home I had built with my own hands was empty when I reached it, and I turned towards my parents' house close by, hoping that Fiona would be there. Sure enough she was; I saw her as soon as I stooped to enter, with my tools on my back, at the low doorway. But before I could cry out a greeting and seize her in my arms, I stopped dead, for my glance had caught my father.

A big man he was by nature, strong and sinewy, as his byname, Uillean Laider, implied, and I suppose he was at this time not more than fifty years of age. I tell you, child, I did not know him when I came home that day. It was a stranger, I thought, who sat there huddled on the *fail-sunk* by the hearth, some wayfarer, maybe, who had been given hospitality. But all the time I knew in my heart that it was my father, though he was shrunken like an old man, his straight shoulders stooped, and his eyes having that blind look you may see in one who has been dealt a heavy blow.

As I stared at him, my sister Moir came hurrying in from the other room, carrying very carefully a black bottle. I knew it well. It was the precious bottle of brandy sent to us, I do not know how many years since, by my mother's uncle when he was serving with his regiment in France. I was sure then that my father had suffered some sudden illness, and began to ask questions, but no one answered me. Then I turned my eyes and saw my mother.

Proud she was, as I have often told you, and never had she grown accustomed to this poor new home, becoming very silent, and setting her lips tight as though she feared what she might say, did she open them. Only once, when news had come that William Og had fallen in battle, had she burst forth against the broken promises of Herself, and the tame way in which the Namhairich had allowed themselves to be driven from Strath Naver without offering resistance.

But she was loyal through and through, and now I saw that she had nothing in her heart but compassion for her man. She knelt there beside him on the earthern seat, rocking him against her breast as though he had been her little child, and caressing him with her hand so gnarled by constant toil. But he seemed not to know that she was there, nor did he give me any greeting, only stared into the fire with vacant eyes so that I trembled, fearing that his reason must have been taken from him along with his bodily health.

While Moir tried to persuade him to taste a sip of brandy, my wife beckoned me into the byre, which made one with the house.

'It was yesterday,' she told me in a low voice, 'that Iain Mackay, he who used to be Sellar's under-shepherd, went to the new Factor's office at Rhives to pay his rent; so timid is

Iain, he will always be beforehand in payment, as you know. He came back white as death. Mr Gunn, the Factor, had bidden him inform his neighbours that the rent for the next half-year would not be demanded, because Herself had decided to clear the whole west side of Strath Naver, from Mudale to the sea, next Whitsunday, and lay it under sheep.'

There arose in me at that the blind red fury I had known when I witnessed the evictions in Strath Naver. It had lain there among the roots of my heart ever since, like a peat fire smoored for the night; and so had my boyhood resolve to make this outrage known to all the world. But it had been damped down by the helplessness that had fallen on us all when Sellar got off scot-free at his trial; what could simple folk do against this alien law, when all were in a conspiracy to protect one of their legal brethren?

Now I felt as I had done on one mad occasion when I was but a boy, and I had risked my life to rob an eagle's nest because Iolair Mor, as we called that bird, had stolen my mother's ewe lamb. For the first time then I had seemed to understand the meaning of the words oppression and injustice, and there had been no room in my passionate soul for the thought that it was folly to feel thus about the natural instincts of a bird of prey.

But now I knew that there was a human bird of prey, whose fine eyrie was in London; and if I could have laid my hands upon some gunpowder, I do believe I would have marched to her ancestral castle of Dunrobin and levelled it with the ground!

For what most enraged me was the betrayal of my father's trust. It was that blow which had turned him into an old man overnight. His faith in her had been unshakeable; he thought of her still, I believe, as the little girl to whom his own father had taken our gifts during her childhood in Edinburgh, who had run to meet her clansman, greeting him in the Gaelic, sending kind messages to all of us her people. Through the long years she had never come to visit us, but always my father had excused it, reminding us of the sad memories haunting Dunrobin, carefully noting on the fly-leaves of the Shorter Catechism the births of her children, praying for her every night, exclaiming sometimes when he was moved, 'May my Chief have the ascendant!', in the old fashion of our race. Not a word would he ever hear against her, blaming all the misfortunes which had befallen us on Patrick Sellar and his kind.

But Sellar was gone from his post; he could no longer serve as a scapegoat. A strange thing my mother had said before we flitted from our dear home in Strath Naver came back to me now:

'Mind you our old proverb, Uillean, "He is a foolish man who thinks he can appease a wolf".'

My poor father had thought to appease a Highland proprietor by doing as he was bidden and removing peaceably; but the predatory instincts of this wolf would not be satisfied until it had taken from us all we had, and scattered us to the four winds of heaven.

Pitiful it was to hear my father, when he came to himself a little, try to find a new whipping-boy for what our Chief was doing; it was this 'foreign' Marquis, her husband, he insisted, who would be driving us out into the wilderness again. But the dogged loyalty of him could not assuage the hurt he had suffered from her who ought to have had the same care for us as a mother for the children of her body.

When notices to quit were handed in at every house throughout twenty-eight miles, our folk did nothing, not this time because they refused to believe that they must flit, but because there was nothing they could do at all. For on this occasion no lands had been lotted to us; we were simply to be smoked out like vermin to the inhospitable coast, where we must live as best we could, or drown our sorrows in the sea. The Namhairich fell back upon a sort of fatalism; what must be, must be.

I beat my head against this apathy, as against a stone wall. I knew that in other parts of the Highlands where there had been resistance to the clearances, the people had been allow-

8

ed to remain. In my travels as a mason I had even been to these parts, and I had heard at the first-hand how women and old men had charged the Sheriff's officers with sticks and burnt the orders of eviction; and I urged on our folk to stand out against aggression even as our forefathers had defied the Norsemen and the might of Rome. But a diet of nettle-broth is very cooling to the blood, and that had become our staple food these last few years.

A fortnight before we were due to quit, Mr Mackenzie preached us a farewell sermon in the open air beside the river. He was a man who, as I have said, was ever very anxious to stand in well with the landlords, and by harping on the old string that we were being punished for our sins he had just been given money enough to send his eldest son to the University, a dear ambition of every minister, and other favours had been showered upon him.

But I will do him the justice to record that on this occasion he was moved to tears, that he preached to us in Gaelic from the text, 'By the waters of Babylon we have sat and wept', and that in drawing a picture of Heaven he assured us that the tooth of the big sheep, which was the root of all our sorrows, will not be seen there.

I will not harrow you, Donald Og, by telling you much about this second eviction. Not one single penny was paid us for the little improvements we had made; we were given half an hour to quit, and then all our homes were burnt. Three hundred houses were in flames at once, and the smoke was so dense that a boat lost her way as she approached the shore, but at night was enabled to reach a landing-place by the light of the conflagration, which lasted six whole days.

I can still hear the horrible hiss as they drowned the peats upon my own hearthstone, and the screams of an old woman who had been confined to a chair for years, and now forced to stand upon her feet. This time we were driven out without benefit of our waygoing crops; and what was worst of all to me was to see Patrick Sellar present. He had got one of the new huge sheep-farms which were to be formed on our land,

and though he had no longer any official power, it was he rather than Factor Gunn who presided over the destruction.

How much do you remember, I wonder, Donald Og, of the place where you were born? Not very much, I hope, for it could not be called a home.

It was at Strathy Point we settled, on the extreme north coast, a spot useless to the proprietors and never designed by Providence for human habitation. The sea was forced up through crevices to a prodigious height, scattering spray and destroying all we tried to grow; and the patches of soil were so scanty that if a dispute arose over them, a man could carry away the patch he laid claim to in a creel on his back and deposit it somewhere else. When one dug, another had to stand and hold the soil up with his hands, or otherwise it would have rolled down into the sea.

There were no shrubs or trees, nothing to break the force of the wind that blew incessantly from Iceland. Our few weak cattle often stumbled over the cliffs and perished, and others strayed to their old pasture-grounds, do what we would to prevent it, where the shepherds immediately impounded them, without food or water, till trespass was paid. It was nothing strange to see the pin-folds, of twenty or thirty yards square, filled to the entrance with shelties, cows and goats for nights and days together in this starving state, trampling on and goring each other. Their owners who had no money (and they were the majority) were obliged to redeem them at the price of their bed and body clothes, or with such little valu-ables as they had been able to save from the two evictions.

It was in this way that my mother parted from her silver-handled *cuoch*. Och! how she had always treasured that heir-loom, but now she had nothing else with which to pay tres-pass. William Og's money, which he had sent home regularly from his pay before his death in battle had long been spent. When my mother came back from redeeming her one poor cow, which was so weak that she must half support it in her arms, she said to me that the only material treasure left her was the letter from the Colonel of my brother's regiment, describing the valour of his last moments.

'He shed his blood,' said she, 'defending the country from which his family is driven out.'

The bitterest gall it was to her to think of her first-born passing away unseen, like a flower in the desert, believing to the last in the empty promises made by Herself when she wanted volunteers. Almost the last words my mother had heard pass William Og's lips were those of our clan slogan, her last sight of him was when he marched cheerily off against a foe of whom he knew nothing except that it was some enemy of Herself and Scotland.

You might suppose that in our present destitution I was better off, having a craft in my fingers, but I was hard put to it now to get masonry work, for our strength had been sapped by a starvation diet, and strangers were always preferred when there was such work going. We lived at first on shellfish and the eggs of the sea-fowl, and many there were who lost their lives by being caught by the tide, so ignorant were we of the ways of the sea. And so it was that when my old sheltie strayed on to a minister's glebe your mother had to redeem him with that bronze armlet she had worn at her wedding. In any case, she said, her arm had grown so thin that she could not keep it on at all.

I must do this reverend gentleman the justice to record that, so far as I know, he had not followed the practice of the shepherds in working a horse all day and returning it to the pin-fold at night.

It was only to be expected that diseases, hitherto unknown, should afflict us, as consumption, rheumatism, bloody flux and dropsy. But it was none of these plagues, it was a broken heart that put an end to my father; he had never recovered from the shock of trust betrayed. Not a word had passed his lips since that day except to speak of his approaching death, and his mind was anchored to sanity only by the hope of being buried in his native soil with the dust of his forebears. It fretted him sore that he had lost his dead-clothes during the last eviction; in those days they were a most treasured possession, and the first task of a bride was to weave the shrouds of her husband and herself.

Knowing his end to be near, my father kept wandering back to Strath Naver, and often I was having to go in search of him, fearful lest he had been harried by the shepherds' collies, and carrying him home on my back, so frail he had grown.

'Sad news! Sad news!' he said to me on one of these occasions. 'I have seen our once well-attended Mission House reduced to the size of a dovecot, and the timber of it covering the inn at Altnaharra. I have seen the churchyard, where my ancestors are sleeping, filled with tarry sheep, and Mr Sage's study-room a kennel for Robert Gunn's dogs.'

You know that we have always regarded death as the Great Journey, a thing natural and accepted, often mentioned in ordinary conversation without a trace of melancholy; and so now our friends and kinsfolk came to ask my father to convey messages to their departed loved ones. The Minister would not have approved, I suppose, but little we saw of him now. In the old days we had thought nothing of walking six or seven miles to church upon the Sabbath, but now the religion of the Presbyterian Church had lost its appeal for us, and all we had left were our ancient beliefs. There was a ritual of decorous departure, folk coming to take solemn farewell of my father, and to say to him, as it might be:

'If it is permitted, tell my dear wife that I have merely endured this world since she left it, and that I have been kind to every creature she used to cherish, for her sake.'

My mother watched him day and night, being careful that no tear should fall upon his face when she knew that he was dying. It was believed that to bedew the dying with tears caused the departed spirit discomfort on its journey to the eternal abode, and nothing must be done to disturb the sacred rest of the dead. My father spoke not at all, but with his eyes he was always begging us not to bury him in alien soil. I swore to him that he should lie with his fathers in

Strath Naver; and so the day came when he 'changed', as we term it, the lids dropped over his weary eyes as the curtain of cloud at night over my dear Mountain of the Maiden, and all his bewilderment and hurt were hidden for ever from the eyes of men.

With my own hands I made the coffin, of twisted wands of willow, while my mother streaked the corpse, setting on its breast the handful of salt to signify immortality, and prepared what she could for the funeral feast. When this was done she sat apart in the next room, upright and motionless, just bowing her head as each new arrival came to condole with her in a low tone. On the day of the funeral, she rose and went into him again, placing the face-cloth over his face, still without word or tear.

I had found many ready enough to form the funeral procession, but so weak we all were from our miserable diet that the four bearers must be relieved every few yards, though the coffin was as light as a child's. At every spot where we rested, a cairn was started in the old tradition, to which we would be adding a stone when we passed it again, and at our head there walked a piper, solemn and slow, playing the ancient dead-tune, *Ha pill, ha pill, me tuillidh*.

Though our Church has no burial service, it always was the custom for the Minister to be present at the graveside to say some prayers, but not one reverend gentleman would attend my father's funeral, lest he get into trouble with the higher powers. Well it was that none did come, for some of the darker folk-lore of the Highlands had crept back among us; I heard folk whisper fearfully that my father must keep the Watch of the Graveyard until another was buried, and before they were putting him in the earth the bearers would be passing three times sun-wise round the grave. As for me, as I laid the green sods over it, being careful to see there was not the least inequality in them, I was thinking with bitterness that soon the sheep would be nibbling over my father's head.

I saw when I came home that my mother had nailed a sprig of pearlswort above her door to prevent the dead from returning. Ay, we had all grown superstitious right enough.

Now I was left with two families to provide for, my mother and my sister Moir, who was not yet wed, my wife and my baby Donald. I have not mentioned, I think, what befell my elder sister, Laleve. Before we were evicted the second time, there came among us agents from the colonies, urging our young folk to go over there where was land in plenty and work for all. Laleve was one of those who were tempted by their glib tongues, and bound herself to work for a term of years in the Americas in return for her passage. Never have we had word of her since.

I determined, therefore, that to eke out my masonry work, which I could get but seldom, I would learn the art of fishing at sea, so alien to a pastoral people.

One of the favourite excuses made for the evictions had always been that there was plenty sustenance and profit to be got if the crofters would but turn their attention to what was described as 'the bounties of the ocean'. They did not reflect for a moment, those who spoke so, that to us free cultivators of the soil the ways of the sea were quite unknown. No one ever mentioned that the herring were erratic, sometimes never coming near the coasts of Scotland, or that when they came there were plenty expert fishermen from the South to catch them, who had a fishing-station at Wick specially built for them, while we had no pier or harbour, but only wretched natural creeks.

But we were the hardiest race in all the world (otherwise we never would have survived on our starvation diet), and marvellously adaptable, never at a loss for an expedient. We had no boats, and did not know how to build any except the little coracles in which we were wont to sail the lochs, and they would be but as paper boats on that wild ocean, where sudden and hideous storms arose, daunting even to the expert fishermen. Yet now that it was fish or starve, myself and four other young men looked about us for a boat we could get cheap, determining to teach ourselves this new strange art of fishing.

I heard of a craft at Helmsdale, where there was no harbour but some quay walls, and we bargained with the southern fishermen for her.

'And what wad ye be doing wi' a boat, Donald?' one of these Lowlanders asked me, with that accent which we called the quaint English.

I was surprised that he should call me by my name, for I did not know then that 'Donald' was the common name they gave to all Highlanders.

They charged us dear for the boat, though they knew right enough she was unseaworthy and had been laid up for years. No sail we had, no compass or helm, and but three patched oars. Lacking rowlock-pegs, I contrived some from the teeth of an old harrow. Some hand-lines we made also, and fashioning them brought back to me the memory of Cailein Bochd, our poor natural, and how skilful he had been at such things. And so we put to sea, only one of us ever having been upon that strange element before.

All our kinsfolk and friends stood on the stony beach, imploring us not to venture forth, lamenting that they would never see us again, except our drowned bodies; while out at sea the Lowland fishermen sat in their good boats and jeered, expecting any moment to see us all go to the bottom, so clumsy were we. Only my mother, that grand woman, encouraged us. What a night that was! We were numb with cold in the flimsy tartan we were forced to buy, because we could no longer maintain our long-haired sheep; and we were mortal sea-sick besides. And at the end of it not a fish did we catch, though at least we got home safely.

So we must try again, and again, and still we could catch nothing. What was worst of all was to see in the morning light all our folk gathered on the beach where they had slept, ready to drag our poor boat above highwater mark, and eager for the sea-food they hoped we had brought them.

The Lowland fishermen plagued us with their own superstitions. How could we hope to succeed, they demanded, when we had no horse-shoe nailed to the stem of our boat, and what would we be doing whistling when we were out at sea? It was a sure way of bringing on a storm, they said. But at last one of them took pity on us, and explained that hand-lines were useless. He showed us what must be used; they called it a 'trot', and it was a strong cord three hundred yards long, upon which snoods were fastened at intervals of six feet, each with a hook at the end of it, baited with sand-eel or whelk. It must be weighted at either end with a heavy stone, and paid out to lie on the bottom across the run of the fish as they swept in with the flood and out with the ebb.

It was a great labour to make this trot, and we were at it, men, women and children, for days together. It must have a big black bladder attached to one end to show where the line lay. When we hauled it in the first time, we found all our bait gone and no fish on the hooks, and we were near despair. It was only then that our Lowland friend condescended to explain that if the trot was left down too long the crabs and dog-fish would come and take the catch.

Then one day when I had caught hold of the bladder and lifted the stone, I saw something on one of the hooks as they began to come in. I think I never was more pleased in all my life before than when that ugly gurnet with the spikes on him came flapping over the side. But then one of the Lowland fishermen shouted to us from his boat:

'Ye'll no eat the meat frae the heid o' yon fush, Donald. Gin ae body ate the meat frae the heid o' yon fush, he wad be poisoned.'

Groaning with disappointment, we threw back our gurnet. The Lowland fishermen, who delighted in tormenting and bemusing us, had not thought fit to tell us that the body of the gurnet makes fine eating. We had to discover such a thing for ourselves, ay, and many others, as that you must not stand but sit down to haul, if you would not get cramp in the small of your back, that a shark-headed dog-fish must be killed before being thrown overboard, but that what they called a 'saft' cod should be thrown back alive.

Many of our folk were drowned in learning this alien

occupation, but some of us became expert fishermen. Yet this was not the end of our troubles. We could feed our families, but except for the shepherds, who were soon satisfied, we had no market for the surplus, and no means of carrying it to the distant towns while it was still fresh. So always there hung over us the nightmare of finding our rent; we knew well enough by this time that our oppressors would not scruple to evict us, even from this wretched spot, if we got behind with our payments.

When the herring came up in May, we had no rest at all; each time our boats returned the whole population must help to drag them up the steep beach, and down again for the next night's fishing, while the women would be clumsily getting the entrails out and putting the fish into brine, or smoking them on wooden spits; for this too was an art we had taught ourselves. And yet, for all this labour, and for all this new skill of ours, we were lucky if we could scrape together a half-year's rent. It maddened me when I saw in the *Inverness Journal* a notice describing sixty lots of land to be let for a fishing-station, concluding with the words, 'A decided preference will be given to strangers.'

But there was something else I read during those terrible years, something that rekindled in my breast the spark of hope. I was at Wick, trying to sell a creel of smoked herrings, and being jeered at by the regular fishermen for the uncouth way in which the entrails had been nipped out, when in a shop window I saw a book for sale, called *Sketches of the Character, Manners, and Present State of the Highlanders of Scotland*. It is a famous book now, thank God, but newly-published then.

An impulse came upon me to buy it, though I could ill afford the price. Thinks I, I will see what this clever gentleman, Colonel David Stewart of Garth, writes about our poor people. I knew he was a Highland proprietor, and I suspected that he would be excusing what was done by other landlords.

May he forgive me for my rash judgment! His was the first voice raised in our defence. He had first-hand knowledge of the clearances in his own part of the Highlands, and he would be putting the blame for them squarely where it belonged, not on underlings like factors and sheep-farmers, but on the proprietors who preferred fat rents to the welfare of their own clansmen. That book produced a great sensation, and it was followed shortly by another in the same strain, written by Dr James Browne, since famous.

I heard that Patrick Sellar, I suppose at the bidding of the Marquis of Stafford, sought counsel's opinion but was advised against bringing a law-suit against either of these learned and brave gentlemen, whose names should be cherished by all our Gaelic race.

I read those books until I knew them almost by heart, and I longed to do in my plain, unvarnished way what they had done to expose our wrongs. I had witnessed the cruelty and injustice perpetrated on that infamous June day in Strath Naver, and again when we were evicted from our poor new homes. The jury had not believed the eye-witnesses who had given evidence at Patrick Sellar's trial, but maybe now, in consequence of those two books, such testimony would not be dismissed as false or exaggerated. I had done well at school, and could write English fluently, and if only I could draw public attention to our case, so as to promote an impartial enquiry, my end would be attained.

Our oppressors believed that, we being an 'illiterate' people, speaking a language almost unknown beyond our mountains, we could not make our wrongs heard through the length and breadth of the land. Colonel Stewart and Dr Browne had seen the evil results of the evictions, but they had not felt them in their own persons, as I had. To describe what it was like to be driven from one's home, to demand the erasure from the Statute Book of a law which permits men like Sellar to oppress poor folk with impunity, to throw a gleam of light on the present wretched state of my own folk, its causes and its consequences, became my one ambition.

This resolve, which I kept secret in my own breast, supported me through all the trials that beset me, as you shall hear.

13

PRIVATE DIARY OF ELIZABETH, COUNTESS OF SUTHERLAND, 1827

May 1st. Have at long last prevailed on George to allow me my proposed visit to Dunrobin, but am aware that he is still much averse to it.

He warns me that the towns have become as unsafe as the roads in the North, reminding me that it is but a few years since the Government was obliged to send three battalions and the Rifle Brigade to put down the armed strikers at Bonnymuir, and that despite King George IV's gracious visit to Edinburgh soon after his Coronation, intermittent riots have continued.

He himself, says my husband, cannot be expected to accompany me at such a time, when the money crisis is not yet over, and Parliament newly dissolved.

I find to my astonishment that many of my friends envy me my expedition. Scotland has suddenly become *a la mode*, as a result of the novels of Sir Walter Scott, and they take it for granted that the prime objects of my visit are to view Melrose Abbey by moonlight, to drink tea with Sir Walter at Abbotsford, and in general to make a pilgrimage to what they term 'Gothic ruins'. Alas, I very much fear I shall see ruins of another sort, whether I wish to or no, in my native Sutherlandshire.

But I am resolved to go. I have not been there since the many removals; I am growing old, and I must see for myself before I die how my own folk are faring. I must sift at first-hand the conflicting rumours of what has been done. Colonel (now Major-General) Stewart's book, followed so soon afterwards by Dr James Browne's *Critical Examination*, vastly disturbed me, and I must confess that I was not greatly impressed by the paper published by Mr Sellar in which he endeavoured to answer these gentlemen's accusations.

May 14th. Edinburgh. A frightful journey so far. Much regret that I decided to travel part of the way by the new Locomotive. I am sure these railways will never become general, for the human frame cannot endure being borne along at twelve miles an hour by a machine. My unhorsed carriage was loaded on to a truck and twice during the journey was I stranded by the lashings giving way. It was so cold that my copper foot-warmer was useless, and am really surprised that the lower orders, who travel in the roofless third-class carriages, are not frozen to death.

I am shocked by the change in Edinburgh since my childhood there. Except that it did not contain a government, it was then one of the leading capitals of Europe, unequalled for its polished society and its splendid streets and squares. The New Town is still well enough, but the historic Mile has become a slum, the old 'lands' in which the gentry lived now housing each a hundred families, two or even more crowded into a single, vermin-ridden room. I have never seen such drunkenness, and am told that raw whisky, doctored with fusel oil, has become among the lower orders like cheap gin in England.

May 15th. Was entertained yesterday at the Music Hall in George Street by the North British Friends of the West Indian Slaves. Cake and fruit were passed round, while the pipe organ played the *Old Hundredth*, and there was much tea and many speeches. I was acclaimed as an eminent friend of the poor and oppressed for my work for Abolition, and a group of children from the Ragged Schools sang me a touching ditty which ran thus:

> *'I thank the goodness and the grace*
> *Which on my birth have smiled,*
> *And made me in these Christian days*
> *A happy British child.*
> *I was not born a little slave,*
> *To labour in the sun,*
> *And wish I were but in my grave*
> *And all my labour done.'*

Could not help remarking that though these children were well scrubbed and put into new clothes, they had the faces of old people, and were miserably pale and thin. Was assured, however, by a professed humanitarian, Mr Wilson, the owner of a large flax mill in Forfar, that his new machinery offered most suitable employment for children of five years old, and that after their day's toil they had two hours' compulsory education.

The Rev. John Campbell further asserted:

'There is no training for the volatile mind of youth equal to that maintained in our factories.'

Was presented at the conclusion of the tea-drinking with Edinburgh's penny-offering for our poor slaves, and a vast number of red flannel petticoats for the same. (Cannot help wondering whether these are quite suitable for the climate out there?) It is frightful to reflect that my own mother owned a black page-boy.

May 30th. Dunrobin Castle. Arrived here yesterday with an armed escort, it having been explained to me that highway robbery, in my childhood unknown in the Highlands, has become all too common now. The new roads excellent, but an extraordinary lack of traffic on them.

A reception committee was assembled in the courtyard, composed of Commissioner Loch, Factor Gunn, a bevy of ground-officers, several ministers and Mr Patrick Sellar. I would have preferred the absence of the last-named, for though I am assured that all the stories of his atrocities are completely without foundation, from his letters he has appeared to me a somewhat unpleasant sort of man. On acquaintance found this impression confirmed; he has, I am convinced, something of the nature of the cur, equally ready to fawn or to snap.

In the evening a quite splendid entertainment had been prepared in my honour. Mr Sellar recited a tedious long poem he had composed, congratulating me on the improvements and containing the line, 'Recurrent famine from his holds she chased'. Do trust that this is true. A set of elegant neck ornaments was presented to me, towards the cost of which, said Mr Loch, even the humblest of my tenants had subscribed. Was surprised and touched, and, I will confess, not a little comforted. They cannot, surely, be in such a destitute state as described by Major-General Stewart in his book.

I was somewhat hurt, however, not to see any of these lowly folk of mine gathered at Dunrobin to greet me, though Mr Loch assured me that it was only out of modesty that they had absented themselves.

I could not sleep very well last night. All sorts of strange, uneasy fancies kept my head tossing restlessly on the pillows. I had no sense of homecoming; indeed, the country of my birth seemed almost hostile, the mountains brooding darkly, the wind soughing round the castle like a lament.

Dunrobin is said to be the oldest inhabited house in Scotland, built by an ancestor of mine in the eleventh century, and perhaps it has stood too long. Its stones seem to exude the breath of those rude times. The Great Hall, in which my forebears feasted their clansmen, was melancholy with dim portraits and banners spider-web thin, and my group of welcomers filled but a small portion of the vast apartment. Yes, George is right; Dunrobin would be better pulled down and rebuilt in the modern style; at present it is not only uncomfortable, but full of ghosts.

Yet I knew it was none of these foolish fancies that kept me wakeful. I was wounded by my people's failure to come to give me the welcome home.

Heartily wish I had not read Major-General Stewart's book.

June 1st. Took coach early, and drove for many miles along the splendid new roads; it is a little sad, of course, that they have so diminished the grandeur of our scenery, but I must not be sentimental. Much admired the good stout houses, roofed with slate, of the sheep-farmers, the healthy appearance of the farmers' wives, and their fine rosy little children. Mr Loch waxed eloquent upon the improvements which have been made.

'In 1812, my lady,' he remarked, 'there were only two shops upon the whole of your estate. Now there are upwards of one hundred, in nearly all of which shoe-blacking is sold, an unmistakable sign of advancing civilisation. And as an instance of the more refined habits of the farmers, no house is built now without a hot-bath and water-closet (begging your ladyship's pardoning for mentioning such humble offices).'

'And the benefits your ladyship's improvements have brought to the economy of Great Britain as a whole!' chimed in Mr Sellar. 'Why, the *exports* of Scotland alone are now something in the nature of a hundred and eighty thousand fleeces and forty thousand carcases of the choicest mutton.'

I was, however, uneasy and depressed. Many a deserted village I saw from my carriage, and many a ruined cottage, but of their former inhabitants I got not a glimpse. I remarked on this to Mr Loch, who told me that the new roads did not pass through those portions of the estate to which the sub-tenants have been removed.

I spoke then on an impulse, which I fear I shall live to regret.

'It is my pleasure,' said I, 'that a general warning be issued to the former inhabitants of the straths, to meet me at certain stated places on the road, so that I may hear from their own lips how they are faring.'

George has often chided me for being too sensitive. Am sure that he is right, and that I only imagined Mr Loch and the others to have seemed averse from this project.

June 5th. Went upon my proposed tour, and was dreadfully shocked by what I saw.

Groups of people were at the roadside as I had ordered, but when I let down the window and bowed to them, they gave me no more greeting in return than if I had been a stranger, I who am their hereditary Chief! The fantastic notion came into my head that maybe they had thought to see me dressed in tartan, with an eagle's feather in my bonnet, and my piper marching before me! I noticed them staring at my reticule which, as it so happens, is shaped like a Highland sporran, a fashion which has just become the rage in Town.

As for them, their appearance was forlorn and destitute past all description. I could not have believed that this once hardy race of mountaineers could have become so enfeebled; many of them looked as though they were far gone in a consumption. I beckoned several to come up to the carriage, and asked them through the Rev. David Mackenzie (for I have long forgotten the Gaelic) how they were faring, and how the Factor was behaving towards them. I did not hear one complaint. Nevertheless I ordered Factor Gunn to distribute oatmeal, bed linen and clothing to all in need. George will rebuke me for my extravagance, but I could not help it.

At a certain spot on the road the fancy took me to alight. I walked with difficulty to the top of an eminence, whence my eyes were startled to behold a hundred or more hovels clinging to the sides of the cliff for all the world like limpets on a rock.

9

'Is it possible,' I exclaimed, 'that there are human beings living in such places?'

'Oh yes, my lady,' says one of the ministers.

'And can you tell me that they are any way comfortable?' I insisted, at the same time feeling the ill choice of the word.

'Quite comfortable, my lady,' he assured me. 'But I am afraid they are bone idle by nature, and will neither set their hands to improvements nor profit by the bounties of the ocean at their doors. Only this last month I have issued certificates to many now begging in Caithness, to the effect that they are legitimate objects of charity.'

This astounded me, for I am well aware that in the old days there were fewer paupers in the Highlands than anywhere else in Britain. It was considered a point of honour for the better off to assist the destitute, and I remember hearing how my father used to maintain permanently in his house some score of old folk for whom their relatives could not provide. I asked Mr Mackenzie how many persons he had had upon his parish-roll before the removals, but he gave me an evasive reply.

On the way home was exceedingly vexed by Mr Sellar's remarking that the only occasions on which the Gaels had been known to bestir themselves was when they lifted their hands against the lawful government. Reminded him sharply that my great-grandfather had been one of the few Highland Chiefs to declare for the Prince of Orange at the Glorious Revolution; that my grandfather had taken an active part on the Government side in the rebellion of 1745; and that my father had raised the first Fencible Regiment during the scare of French invasion in 1756.

Consider Sellar a perfectly odious sort of man.

June 30th. I am leaving Dunrobin romorrow, having decided to cut short my visit in consequence of the distressing experience I suffered yesterday.

I had entertained some of the neighbouring gentry at dinner, as they still call it here, a heavy meal indeed to have to digest in the middle of the day, though fortunately I had brought my French chef with me. I was taking some needful repose afterwards, when my maid informed me that Mr Loch presented his compliments and begged a word with me. After apologising a thousand times for disturbing my repose, he broke out thus:

'Madam, there is a fellow here, one Donald Macleod, who has been an hour at the castle gate, insisting on seeing your ladyship. Nothing will move him, and therefore I beg that your ladyship may issue a positive command to him through me to be gone about his business.'

Would that I had done so! But (I will confess it between the pages of this diary, since no eyes will ever see it but mine) my conscience had continued to plague me as a result of what I had seen on my tour, and I was determined that if this man Macleod had any just complaint, I would hear it. Mr Loch warned me that the fellow was a known trouble-maker, but I was obstinate. I bade Loch bring him up to my private parlour, and himself to remain in the ante-room throughout the interview, in case I needed him.

The person I found awaiting me in the parlour was a man I should judge to be near thirty years of age, handsome enough in a rugged sort of way, with a tall, upright carriage, though he had the marks upon him of under-nourishment. He wore a shabby moleskin working dress, and stood with his old bonnet in his hand; I sensed, I don't know why, that he expected me to bid him cover his head after he had made his bow to me. For all his uncouth dress, and gnarled, toil-worn hands, he had a curious dignity, I had almost said a regal air, as though he were my equal. Indeed I fancy he made a gesture as though he would shake me by the hand.

It struck me for the first time that I ought to have had an interpreter present, for Macleod greeted me in the Gaelic. But as I moved towards the bell-pull to have one sent for, my visitor said, with a kind of sadness:

'Madam, I must make known to you, by your leave, that I both understand and speak the English tongue. I addressed your ladyship in the language common to our race because I thought you would have preferred it.'

'You have something that you wish to say to me, I believe,' said I, seating myself upon a couch.

He looked directly at me in a somewhat disconcerting fashion, though without rudeness, and began:

'I beg leave to remind your ladyship that we your clansmen have an inbred dislike of making our wants known, and that we will suffer deeply before we will ask for help. So it has ever been.'

'I am aware of it,' said I, 'and it was for that precise reason that I made a tour of my estate early in this present month. I was resolved to see and to hear for myself whether any of my tenants were in want. Though I heard no complaint, I have ordered oatmeal and clothing to be distributed. Pray inform me if there are any needy cases I have overlooked.'

'Your ladyship ordered that these bounties be distributed through your Factor and ground-officers, by your leave,' said he, 'who will feed the meal to their cattle and poultry, so soon as your back is turned, or keep it until it is so rotten that it will be fit only for flinging on the middens.'

I was extremely shocked, not only by what he said but by the quiet bitterness with which he said it. I told him that in making these accusations, he in fact accused me, who had appointed these officers.

He did not seem abashed. On the contrary, he spoke to me with simple earnestness, turning his old worn bonnet in his hands the while in a gesture which had something very touching in it.

'Madam,' says he, 'if your ladyship would but spend only part of each year on your Highland estate, you would soon see for yourself how these officers treat your poor people, who trust you and look to you as their only and natural protectress. It was because they fear and dread the Factor and his underlings that they dared not make any complaint to your ladyship during your tour. I have said that we dislike

making our wants known, but that is only to strangers. And
so I have come to appeal to you in person, by your leave,
when no factors or ministers are by, not for myself but on
behalf of those who, though humble, are your ladyship's own
kith and kin.'

I realised now my folly in having consented to see this
man. I am, as George continually reminds me, romantical
by nature, and am an easy prey to those who have a glib
tongue. I resolved to harden my heart and to speak sensibly.

'I pay you the compliment, Macleod,' said I, 'of addressing you as an intelligent man. Now I am aware that it is
hard for the people here, shut up in the mountains as they
are, to accept innovations, and to adapt themselves to the
progress which is going on in the more civilised portions of
Great Britain. But it is high time you forsook the selfish and
insular attitude of your ancestors and learned to regard
yourselves as members of a nation which is becoming more
glorious and powerful than she has ever been before. I
myself,' I added candidly, 'found it difficult in my youth to
shed certain prejudices inherent in me, but I have acquired
a wider outlook.'

He had listened to me with those penetrating eyes of his
fixed steadily on my face, and replied with some irony:

'I would ask your ladyship, by your leave, if it is progress
when an employer in the South comes to regard his work-
people, not as his men but as his "hands", and whether a
Highland proprietor becomes more enlightened when he
regards *his* people, who share with him a common ancestor,
as a nameless mass to be uprooted, evicted and moved
hither and thither as he pleases, regardless of their comfort.'

I was vexed, and longed to tell him he was being imper-
tinent; but in fact he was not. That constant 'by your leave'
was no empty phrase, for it is true that the Gaels have always
been the politest people in the world. And the memory was
strong in me of how, from ancient times, our clansmen have
been accustomed to pass their joke with their Chief, and to
argue with him, without the slightest offence meant or taken.

I had the most absurd feeling all through the interview that I was on trial before this simple Highland peasant, and that he was giving me my chance—of what I am quite unable to say.

'Macleod,' said I crisply, 'what has been done in the way of removals was done strictly according to law. The trial of Mr Sellar should have convinced you of that. The Marquis, my husband, has the most profound respect for our legal code, and so have I. If there are cases of hardship, it is no longer incumbent upon the proprietor to relieve them since we now have public charity. On the other hand we do not expect from our people the old slavish attitude towards their Chiefs.'

His face hardened, and he said sternly:

'Your ladyship has forgotten, by your leave, that we have no such word as "slave" in the Gaelic tongue. And yet there are some who have fallen to that state when they would rather be well-fed slaves on a West Indian plantation than starved freemen in the Scottish Highlands. The papers are full of praises of your ladyship's philanthropy towards the negroes. I marvel that you can have so much tenderness for strangers in a distant land, and none for those who are your own kinsmen.'

I was very angry at this. For I felt his unspoken comment: Your work for Abolition is a subtle act of conscience. And that is untrue; it is most bitterly unjust!

'I must ask you to mind your manners, Macleod,' I flashed at him.

'I beg your ladyship's pardon if I have offended by my plain speaking,' said he, unabashed, 'but I had understood that you desired to learn the truth about the condition of your people, and that this was why you made your tour of the estate. And I would respectfully ask you who are the greater objects of commiseration—a brave, moral and chivalrous race, who were born free and have defended their freedom through untold ages, or your black slaves who have never tasted liberty? The child born blind is not so helpless as the poor fellow who has been deprived of his sight after arriving at manhood.'

'However that may be,' I retorted, being desirous to end this interview, 'the truth is our Highland glens were over-populated, and in bad seasons the people had not sufficient to eat; this you know as well as I do. The scheme of improvements set in motion by the Marquis and myself was designed for the benefit of these inhabitants, besides the welfare of Great Britain as a whole. Though it is true that you and others have been obliged to vacate the lands to which you were so much attached, it is extremely unjust to say, as some recent authors have done, that thereby we deprived you of all means of support. There is emigration for the young and strong; there is the harvest of the sea contiguous to your new homes; and there is work upon the roads or in the towns. At all events the march of progress is not to be retarded by mere sentiment.'

I rose to indicate that the interview was at an end, but I was arrested in the act by a most strange transformation which had come upon my visitor. I was not alarmed by his changed aspect, for I was sure he had forgotten my presence. It was not to me that he spoke now with such passion, his dark eyes glowing, his voice vibrating, but to some intangible enemy. There were no longer any "by your leaves".

'Deprive us of our natural livelihood and steal from us the lands our fathers have occupied from time beyond counting, and you will not find us hiring ourselves out to make roads and bridges for those who have supplanted us. If you find us upon this earth at all, which God created for the use of all who bear His image, it will be in the South, swelling the hordes of beggars on the highway, or toiling among the bond-slaves in your factories. There we shall be unknown, unnoticed among a multitude of ruined peasants, out of sight of our native hills from which we have been driven to make way for sheep, and of the reproachful ghosts of our freedom-loving fathers.'

He took a step towards me, his hands clenched upon his

bonnet; and still, though I would gladly have silenced him, I did not fear him.

'Misery, pauperism, demoralisation,' he raged, 'these are the fruits of your boasted improvements. Sons of little men, sycophants like Sellar, harp upon the string that we Gaels are bone idle, but no agricultural people are by nature indolent. Yet, take from them that which gives them self-respect and an incentive to labour, steal from them their human dignity by transforming them from small owners into a mob of unwanted refugees, push them around as a nuisance to beg their bread from the public purse, and they will be as idle as their broken hearts have made them, and like your dispossessed southern peasants they will become inmates of jails and food for gallows.'

I was astonished by the eloquence of this poor working man. I felt my face flush with shame as I recognised at least some truth in his accusations. It seemed to me that he had become the very embodiment of my ancient race; that it was by them I had been tried, and found wanting.

Then he seemed to become aware of my presence again, and though there was no hostility in his eyes, there was no longer appeal. He spoke with that reserved politeness with which the Gael will address a stranger.

'I beg your ladyship's pardon,' he said again, 'for laying by for a time the manners of a Highland gentleman. And I offer your ladyship my thanks for making the situation plain to me. I came to appeal to *Ban Mhor fhear Chat*, our natural mother and protectress. But I understand now that she no longer exists. There is only our landlord, the Lady Marchioness of Stafford.'

He bowed to me at that, and left the room before I could say another word.

Memo. To be sure to leave it in my will that these diaries be burnt unopened at my decease.

14

LETTER FROM PATRICK SELLAR TO THE MARQUIS OF STAFFORD

MUDALE FARM, Sutherlandshire, North Britain. July 1st, 1827.

I beg a thousand pardons for troubling your lordship with these few lines, but feel it incumbent upon me, on behalf of all on the Sutherland Estate, to express our gratitude for the gracious visit of the Lady Marchioness, who parted from us today. She came like an angel of light into a dark wilderness, shedding her beneficent beams even into its remotest corners, and upon the humblest of its denizens.

My one regret is that a fellow named Macleod, blacklisted by me for some years as a trouble-maker, forced himself into her ladyship's presence at the end of her stay, and, I am afraid, discomposed her ladyship's tender heart by his impudent complaints. I had already warned Mr Loch concerning him and now have spoken to Factor Gunn that he should take the first opportunity to have this mischievous Radical turned off the estate.

There are others who, though they do not venture to complain, we would be well rid of. I do not deny that they have the image of the Almighty on their countenances, but in intellect they are little above the condition of the brute creation. Yet even for these there would be some hope if they could be induced to emigrate. It is, my lord, I sincerely believe, the sovereign remedy for the still over-populated Highlands.

Take an indolent Celt, let him go to America, and he

becomes industrious; take a wild Irishman, he becomes civilised; take a blind, bigoted Papist, his eyes are opened and he turns his back on Rome. These are facts extraordinary; we pour with many good elements a singular amount of impurity across the Atlantic, but America does not cast it off, it merges, changes, and reforms it, like the sea that receives many muddy rivers, but keeps its own bosom clean.

But these cases I have mentioned are, I am happy to say, the exception. In general, from being indolent and vicious, the tenants have become paragons of industry and virtue. They have at length put by their ridiculous prejudice against that wholesome food, the fish, and have learnt to catch the finny tribe; and, marvellous to relate, they begin to appreciate the benefits of education.

One seldom meets with a peasant's son of this district nowadays who has not, from the slender wages of his parents, been taught to read, write, and cast up an account. If a tolerable proficient, away he goes to seek his fortune, but go where he may, his heart is with his father's house, and if he succeeds in life, which he generally does to a certain extent, the inmates there are the better for it. The parent wrestles hard to push forward some part of his family by dint of education; the child

> Deposits his hard-won penny-fee
> To help his parents dear,
> Should they in hardship be.

All this is a result of your lordship's improvements in this county, and among a people hitherto notorious for their barbarism and ignorance.

By reciprocal good offices, by joint industry, sobriety and prudence, they now get on wonderfully. In sickness they apply at the nearest shepherd's house where any medicine or comfort is likely to be obtained (for they have overcome to a large extent their absurd native pride); and for the least drop of honey, jelly, wine or even vinegar there is a visit from the patient as soon as he can crawl abroad, with a thousand thanks and a little gift of dried herring or shellfish, which how to refuse, or pay for without giving offence, it requires some tact to discover, for they are still ridiculously touchy.

It is in vain, I fear, to impress upon them that they must not help themselves to the cockles and mussels, these delicacies being prized on the tables of persons of refined tastes; and Mr Loch has been obliged to appoint a Mussel Bailiff and to post armed constables along the coast to prevent this theft of shellfish.

On entering the habitation of the cottar, his fare is found to be very simple. It is fish, either fresh or dried, with potatoes and oatmeal porridge if the weather has been so propitious as to allow these commodities to grow, with the addition in winter of a kind of soup which they make from the seaweed called dulse. Their abstinence from tea, coffee, sugar, wheaten flour and flesh meat is entire. I must add also, I am afraid, from soap! That this very meagre diet is not incompatible with long life, health and strength, is proved by the fact that two peasants who entered my service as day-labourers on my farm of Culmailly, are now, at the age of over eighty, still doing some light work about the farm.

In fine, my Lord Marquis, the Highland peasant, unlike the Cheviot sheep, will thrive on anything. In a hard winter I have known the former to subsist for months on frozen potatoes dug out of the snow.

In my humble opinion, the improvements made on this estate by the noble proprietors afford an almost sublime instance of the benevolent employment of superior wealth and power in shortening the struggles of advancing civilisation, and elevating in a few years a backward people to a point of education and material prosperity which, unassisted, they could never have attained.

15

DONALD MACLEOD'S STORY
concluded

I AM approaching now, Donald Og, that portion of my tale in which you shared, and though you were not yet eight years old when it happened, fear is on me that such an experience must have left a scar on your young mind. But wait you till I relate what led up to it.

It was soon after the visit of the Marchioness of Stafford to Dunrobin that we folk who had been driven to the sea-coasts received each of us a notice from Commissioner Loch. He told us it was her ladyship's pleasure that all the sub-tenants from Bighouse to Melness (a stretch of thirty miles), build new houses with stone and mortar according to a prescribed plan and specification. The reason given was that her ladyship deemed the little sod cabins we had contrived for ourselves on that barren coast to be 'insanitary and unfit for human habitation'.

We were appalled by this order, not only because we had a prejudice against stone walls as being cold, but because when finished these new houses would have cost between thirty and forty pounds apiece, a huge sum for those who had no livelihood now except the uncertain harvest of the sea. Some got up petitions and sent them to her ladyship, but the only answer she returned was that those who did not immediately begin to build would be removed at the next term.

The dread word "removed" was enough for us; while we could stay on our native earth, though it be only on the uttermost fringe of it, we would somehow manage. It was the same when her ladyship's intention to visit us had been announced, and Factor Gunn came round to seek subscriptions for a handsome set of ornaments for her neck. His ominous shake of the head, and his murmur of that word "removal", had made the most destitute hasten to give him something, though it must be from the few pounds they had scraped together for a decent funeral.

I was a skilled stonemason, and offered to Mr Loch my services free for my kinsfolk and friends. But not at all! There must be strange masons and squads of mechanics from the South fetched up, whom our folk must feed and pay, and for whom they must fetch and carry. The timber was supplied by Commissioner Loch, who charged us two-thirds higher than the price they were asking in the neighbouring sea-ports.

All must work to build these whited sepulchres, in which we were to starve more uncomfortably than in our old warm turf cabins; and even when built, we had no security of retaining them. I saw my own mother trundling clay and wood upon a barrow, her tracks reddened with her blood from hands and feet. I saw my aged father-in-law trying with trembling hands to raise stones to the walls; and my lovely wife, your mother, then great with her fourth child, bowed almost double by the heavy creel of lime upon her back. It was the herring season, when a night lost meant we could not make up our rents, so that the young men must spend all the dark hours fishing, and the light ones at the quarry.

This new oppression killed my mother, as a second eviction had put an end to my father. Handling the strange material she fell, and got a great hurt in her leg which would not heal.

A grand woman to the last was Christian Stewart; royal was her race indeed! Not one murmur passed her lips at the great pain she suffered, though when my sister Moir would be raising her up in bed to give her drink, I have seen the sweat start out all over her face with the anguish. On the day when she "changed", she was speaking to me words I never have forgotten.

'Do you remember,' she asked me, 'what our hero Galgacus said to our forebears when they faced the Roman legions upon the Mount of Battle? "To ravage, to slaughter, to usurp under false pretences, these men call empire; and where they have made a desert, they call it peace." You were born too late to draw the sword against oppression, my son; but you have a pen.'

I knew then that she had guessed what I was doing, when she saw a fir-candle burning in my house at a time when I should have been in my bed. She read now my answer in my eyes, and she gave me a glorious smile, murmuring:

'That's you!'

So little time then there was for mourning the dead, that on the very day of her funeral I walked fifteen miles to Factor Gunn's farm, because I had heard he was rebuilding his sheep-cot, and I would be bargaining with him to get the stones from his old one cheap to help in the erection of the house I was ordered to put up for my family.

He was a Caithness man, but his family had lived long in the Lowlands, and he had the strange accent of those parts. A decent man he was, though weak enough to do anything to please the higher powers. I suppose he saw in my face (for I had not the cash even for a black riband in my bonnet) that I had suffered some bereavement; at anyrate, when I was asking him would he sell me the old stones, he patted me on the arm quite kindly, and said och, they were but rubbish and I was welcome to them, if I could carry them away.

But so suspicious had I grown of kindness, like a dog long ill-treated, that I growled at him and said I did not ask for charity.

'Weel then, Donald,' says he, 'let's no argy-bargy aboot sic a trifle, but gi'e me a siller shillin', and shift yersel oot o' the way, for I've wark tae dae.'

I could not believe in my good fortune; and because I

knew from painful experience how, unless you had something in writing, they could catch you with their legal tricks, I asked him if he would please to give me a paper saying he had let me have this stone for a shilling. He upbraided me with what he called my ingratitude, but at last he gave me a receipt, which I put up very carefully in my father's old sporran.

Every day after that I would be walking over to his farm to fetch away the stone in a barrow, for none of us now could keep a sheltie-beast. I was busy at this toil one morning, when there came out to me Iain Mackay, he who had been one of Sellar's shepherds, and now had got a post as constable.

'Donald,' says he, not looking me in the eyes, 'Mr Gunn has sent me to fetch you to his office.'

I wondered much what such a summons could mean, but I was not long left in doubt. The Factor was sitting at his table in his office, with a baton laid beside the ink-well as a sign that he was in his magisterial capacity, for he was a Justice of the Peace.

'Donald Macleod,' he rapped out very sharply, 'ye owe me five pun, eight shillin's, for stane ye ha'e been takin' frae ma sheep-cot.'

I stared at him in a sort of stupor.

'You are mistaken, sir, by your leave,' said I. 'Mind you how you were good enough to let me have the stone for a shilling, after you had offered it to me free, and here is your receipt for that sum.'

'Hoot toot!' says he in high scorn. 'D'ye think me daft? Near upon a ton o' braw stane ye ha'e been carrying awa this fortnight syne, which the appraiser has valued at five pun, eight shillin's. Noo, will ye pay yon debt, or maun I pursue ye for it?'

'I thought you were my judge, sir,' said I.

'I'll baith pursue and judge ye,' he snarls at me. 'John Mackay, seize the defender.'

Poor Iain looked at me imploringly, thinking, I suppose,

that I would make resistance. But I walked of my own accord into an adjoining room, for I was wanting to probe this mystery by myself. It was hard to believe that the Factor would have played me such a trick, for as I have told you, he was a decent man. But then I began to wonder, was he acting under orders? I knew that on the occasion of the visit of the Marchioness of Stafford I had brought down upon my head the wrath of those who administered the estate, ay, and perhaps her own for my plain speaking to her at Dunrobin. Was Mr Loch, I wondered, using this pretext to have me rooted out? But still I could not credit that he would stoop so low; and besides, I had my receipt. Ach, I had such trust in that little bit of paper!

Mr Gunn kept me locked up for more than two hours, and then he summoned me back to the bar.

'Weel, mon,' says he, 'what ha'e ye got to say the noo? Will ye pay this money?'

'Just the same as before you imprisoned me, sir,' I answered. 'I deny the debt. Your receipt proves that I have paid what you asked for the old stones.'

With that he lost his temper, or at least he seemed to do so, perhaps to give himself confidence. At anyrate he seized his baton and banged upon the table with it, as he raged:

'A receipt for ane shillin', for which I was letting ye tak' ane barrowful of stane, and ye expecting ye could ha'e a whole ton o' it! Ye're the damnedest rascal e'er I kent, but if ye ha'e the sum pursued atween Heaven and Hell, I'll gar ye pay it, and I'll ha'e ye ooted frae the estate.'

'Mind you, sir,' I warned him, 'that you are in your magisterial capacity.'

'I'll let ye ken that fine!' he bellowed, and gave me a volley of oaths for good measure.

My own anger was now roused, and I said to him fiercely:

'Sir, your conduct disqualifies you for your office, and under the protection of the law, and in presence of this court, I put you to defiance!'

He let me go, but I knew well enough he had not done

with me. As I went home, I puzzled in my mind should I tell my wife what had passed, and I decided that I would not, she being near her time, and having so much to trouble her already.

But when I came into our little house that evening, I saw at once that she was in one of her fey moods. She was standing by the table with her back to me, and she did not turn at my entrance. She was steeping husks of corn to make the dish called skilling, poor sustenance indeed, but it made a change from the everlasting fish. Suddenly she said to me, still without turning, and in a strange, breathless kind of voice:

'We never shall be living in that grand new stone house we have been breaking our backs to build.'

I felt a shudder of superstitious fear go through me. She had spoken with such conviction; and yet she could not have known what had passed between myself and Factor Gunn.

'My dear white heart,' said I, cheerfully as I could, 'I will have it ready for us in another month whatever, and fine it will be for the little one who is coming to us, for there shall be an upper room snug under the roof——'

She interrupted me. She was staring straight before her, and she said in a tone of dull, resigned despair:

'While you were absent today, I saw the *tamhasg* of a man come to this door and nail it up. There were others with him, and I could not see their faces, but I heard the hiss of water on the hearthstone, and I felt the cold wind blow about my homeless children.'

I was confounded by her words. I had often suspected that she had the two-sights, and from all that I had ever heard such dread visions always were fulfilled. But I pushed that thought away from me and tried all I knew to comfort her, though there was plenty dread in my own breast when I thought of Factor Gunn and the dirty trick he had played me. I sat with my arms about my dear wife, giving her what silent consolation I could, for there were no words in me then. So still it was, as we sat there beside the fire; the tide was out and there was no sound of wind or wave; the even breathing of my children beyond the wicker partition only intensified the silence.

Then, from some distance away, melancholy in the darkness, there came the crowing of a cock.

'It is near to morning,' I muttered, rising and stretching my cramped limbs, 'and you and I, my heart, have had no sleep. When the bright daylight comes again, you will be forgetting your ill visions.'

But Fiona sat motionless, huddled in her plaid.

'It is not near to morning,' she said fatefully. 'It is scarcely midnight, and cocks that crow at such unseasonable hours foretell calamity.' Then she drew a long, shuddering breath, and again she repeated, deep in her throat: 'I felt the cold wind blow about my homeless children.'

For me, at least, the blessed light of morning brought new confidence, and I turned my mind to practical measures.

First I prepared a humble memorial of my case for the Marchioness of Stafford, stating exactly what had passed in conversation between the Factor and myself when I went to bargain with him for the old stones, and promising that I would answer the accusations of my enemies by undeniable testimonies of honest and peaceful character. This memorial I took to the post office at Golspie.

While I waited for a reply, I set about getting signatures to a certificate of character, and naturally I approached the Minister first. He made no objection, but said that he was busy just then and that I must send my wife for it next day. But that same evening, as I learned afterwards, Factor Gunn had the Minister to supper, and the Rev. David Mackenzie sent word to me next morning that my wife need not trouble herself to come, because he had changed his mind and could not sign the certificate. This was a dreadful blow to me, for I knew well that little attention would be paid to such a document unless it had ecclesiastical sanction.

I had been out all night at the fishing and was dead tired, but now I had got it into my head that there was some plot against me, and I must probe it to the bottom. Hearing that the Minister was gone to catechise with his Elders at Helmsdale, thither went I, without pausing for bite or sup, and marched boldly into the house where they were.

They were propounding the question, 'What is the Tenth Commandment?', and before I could stop myself, I cried in a sort of frenzy:

'It is, "Thou shalt not covet", and I would have it written in big letters and sent to every Highland proprietor who covets his poor people's lands.'

Mr Mackenzie tried to push me outside, but I said to him:

'No, sir, not at all. I wish what passes between you and me to be before witnesses. I want a certificate of my moral character, or else an explanation from you before your Elders why it is withheld.'

My old father-in-law was present, and he began to be earnest with the Minister to sign, and some of the other Elders seconded him.

'I would favour you on your late father's account, Donald Macleod,' says the Minister, 'and much more on your father-in-law's, but you are at variance with the Factor, and your conduct is unscriptural, for you obey not those who are set in authority over you.'

Not a word about the pretended debt! I was put into such a passion by his evasiveness and the mesh in which I was being entangled, and so light-headed with fatigue and hunger, that I fairly roared at him:

'I do believe that if my father and my father-in-law, whom you have mentioned with so much respect, stood at the gate of Heaven seeking admittance, and nothing but a false accusation on the part of some of the factors to prevent them, you would join in refusing their entrance to all eternity!'

'You are a Satan,' he raged at me, 'and not fit for human society! Be gone out of this house, or I will put the Church censure on you.'

I had done myself no good by my loss of self-control, though there was excuse enough for my passion. Home I went, and despairing of Mr Mackenzie's signature now, I began to collect others to my certificate of character. So many did I get, and among them Elders and Deacons, that their names filled full four pages; and while things stood thus, I had an answer to my memorial.

Not from the Marchioness of Stafford to whom I had addressed it. It was Mr Loch who wrote to me, saying he would be up in Sutherland in September, and would investigate my case. The day I received this letter, my fourth child was born, my little Uillean; it seemed to me a good omen that I should have heard from Mr Loch on that day, for he wrote to me quite kindly.

But my wife would not be comforted. In her weak state her grand courage had deserted her, and she was a prey to every sort of superstition. She checked me sharply when I remarked upon the beauty of my infant son; since I had done so without first invoking the Deity, I had left the child at the mercy of the evil eye. And because it would be long before he could be baptised she would have me fetch water from under a bridge, carrying it dumb and sprinkling it over the little one in the name of the Three Blessed Persons. Ay, and she must have nails driven into the bed-board, and the smoothing-iron placed in the window, lest the fairies came to steal her babe; the midwife must wind a straw rope about him to protect him from the falling-sickness, and the old wives must watch about her for eight nights.

Yet I do not think it was the People of Peace she was fearing; the visions she had seen nailing up her door were those of human men.

Near the end of September, Iain Mackay came to summon me to the Factor's office, and here I found Mr Loch, with Gunn and some ground-officers standing behind his chair.

'Well, Mr Macleod,' began the Commissioner briskly, 'why don't you pay this five pounds, eight shillings, for which you are being pursued?'

This was a bad beginning, for I had explained most carefully in my memorial the matter of the Factor's old stones. I showed Mr Loch my precious bit of paper, the receipt I had, but he waved it aside and continued:

'Will you pay it all together, or by instalments?' And then, before I had time to answer, he suddenly leaned forward and shot at me: 'If you are allowed to stay on the estate.'

I would not fall into so plain a trap, or let myself be blackmailed. Instead, I handed to him my certificate of character. He seemed taken aback by the number of signatures upon it, but said quickly:

'I cannot see the Minister's name here. How is that?'

'I applied to the Minister, sir,' I said, 'but he would not sign it whatever.'

'Why?' asked Mr Loch, smiling rather unpleasantly.

'He stated as his reason that I was at variance with the Factor,' I replied.

'That is bad,' said Mr Loch gravely. 'However, I will wait upon Mr Mackenzie and hear what he has to say.'

'Will you, sir,' I asked, 'allow me to meet you and Mr Mackenzie face to face when he gives his reasons for not signing?'

'Bless me!' exclaimed the Commissioner, appearing very shocked. 'Will you not believe what he says?'

'I have too much reason to doubt it, sir,' said I. 'But if he attempts to take away my character, I hope you will allow him to be examined on oath.'

'By no means,' said Loch coldly. 'We must surely take the word of the Minister.'

But then he suddenly turned kind and soothing.

'Do you go quietly home, Mr Macleod,' said he, 'and about your business. Be sure to have your new house finished within the stated time, get in your peats as usual for the winter, and before I go south again I will let you know the result of my investigation.'

I did not know what to make of it all. There was still a suspicion in my mind that I was the victim of some plot, yet surely, thought I, the Commissioner would hardly have bidden me get in my winter peats if he intended turning me out. I finished the building of the new stone house, which must stand to air before we moved into it; and then because, like the rest of our folk, I had got myself into debt to buy the timber and pay the mechanics, I walked the long miles to Wick where I had heard there was some masonry work to be got.

I obtained the work there, and that made me more cheerful. But when I returned to my lodging in the town on the night of October 20th, I was so restless that I could not sleep. I told myself it was just the weather; the air had become piercing cold that afternoon, and the wind had risen. I could hear it now, shrieking through the streets and moaning in the chimney, and the breakers on the shore made an awesome accompaniment, full of menace. Winter had come early, and thinks I, there will be an on-ding of snow before morning, ay, the corries will be flat with the braes.

Tossing and turning in my bed, my mind was full of the thought of home. In such a storm, our frail little cabins might be torn from the cliffs like birds' nests; so I argued with myself, though I knew that they had stood now many a winter, and that it was not the weather that made me long to set off there and then to see if all was well with my loved ones.

No, I had become infected with my wife's fears, and as allies to them there were my own. My friendless state in that strange town, and the hour of the night when the spark of life is low, increased my anxiety to a state of panic. I was sure now that some mean plot had been hatched against me from the time when I got the stone for a shilling from Factor Gunn, and that if evil were intended, they would make it both sudden and secret.

I saw them all in a conspiracy, the Marchioness of Stafford, who was no longer Herself but a stranger who cared nothing for us, Commissioner Loch, the Minister, ay, even Patrick Sellar. Sellar was the kind of man of little soul who would nurse revenge in his bosom; he would be wanting to take it out of somebody for his public trial. It was true that he had been acquitted, but for all that his name had become so hated throughout Scotland that he had been obliged to resign the factorship.

But then I thought I was letting my imagination run away with me. Could any gentleman of honour (and such I supposed Mr Loch to be) lull his victim into a sense of false security, and then take vengeance on a defenceless woman with an infant at her breast? So I tortured myself, now one way, now another; but all the time it was as if the very air I breathed were charged with evil, and that in the gale I heard my wife's voice calling to me for help.

At last I could stand it no longer. It was yet early in the night, and if I hastened I could make home by morning. I rose and dressed myself, and leaving my heavy tools behind that I might walk the faster, I set off for Strathy Point. As I left the outskirts of the town, the first snowflakes stung my lips with ice.

I cannot tell you how it was with me upon that walk across Caithness, only that I was like a drunken man, or else the very earth seemed leagued against me. I knew the way well enough, and in spite of all these years of near starvation, I was still strong and active. Yet my feet sank into morasses which should not have been there, the hills assumed strange shapes as though I were traversing an unknown country, the snow was full of little hands to blind me, and the tempest, that familiar winter visitant, scourged me as with whips.

Old beliefs affected me; it was dangerous to be out alone when the sun had gone to sleep, for the night was given over to the Still Folk and other supernatural beings; I wished I had brought my tools with me after all, cold iron being always considered a protection. Then again I would curse myself for a fool; and next moment it would be with me as it is in nightmare, my limbs seeming to have no power in them to move. My grief! the night was possessed by a demon right enough, and the powers of Hell rode on the gale.

The light in the east came tardily, and showed me a

desolate scene indeed. I was miles still from my home, and feared that I had been walking in circles. Yet even at such a time, and in such a state, boy, my spirits rose in answer to the beauty of my land, though it was the loveliness of desolation. The snow had ceased falling, and I walked upon a soft white carpet which merged into the faint grey sky on every hand; down in a gorge I saw a more vital transparency, where the river fell in thundering cascades, edged by tall grasses which the ice had enclosed in little glassy suits of armour. The poetry of my race, in which my mind had been steeped from boyhood, came flowing through, washing away all the panic of the night.

Then suddenly I saw, a long way off but moving towards me, two human figures, black against the snow. They seemed to be blown in my direction from the heart of the storm.

I began straightway to run to meet them, feeling the hair on my nape creep and a shudder seize me. For I knew then, not knowing how I knew, that some evil had befallen those I loved. I knew it beyond all doubting, I say, long before I reached those figures, and looked into the face of my wife. Ochon, child, it was the face of one from whom the reason had fled.

Her companion told me briefly what had happened, having to shout it at me, the gale making a roaring accompaniment, like some demon minstrel. The name of this Good Samaritan (which has been in my prayers ever since) was William Innes, and he was a sheep-farmer of Sandside in Caithness. All the while he was speaking I gazed in blanched horror at my poor wife; she groped continually with her hands, as though she sought to find again the reason lost to her for ever.

Mr Innes told me, then, that my wife and children had been evicted from our home last evening, and that she, after trying in vain to induce a neighbour to take them in, had left her babes with her plaid as covering, and had set off walking to the bounds of the estate. Instinct told her, I suppose, that only when she was off the Sutherland property would she find someone to assist her. But by God's providence, she had not gone far on her way, when she encountered my dear old schoolmaster, Donald Macdonald, who, disregarding the risk to himself, had opened his door to her, given her some refreshment, and taken her to Mr Innes's farm.

'There is an empty house of mine,' says Mr Innes to me now, 'at Armadale, not many miles from your old home, to which I am escorting her, and which you are free to occupy, Mr Macleod, for as long as you need it, though I must warn you that it stands within the Sutherland Estate.'

At that moment I was in a fit mood for a deed that would have served as a future warning to Highland tyrants; ay, red murder was in my heart, may God forgive me. But the poor vacant eyes of my wife, and the hope of yet saving my children, stayed my hand. Leaving Fiona in the care of her protector, I set off at a run, and never paused for breath till I reached what had been our home.

My sorrow! It was a poor place enough at the best of times, but now it stood there like a violated tomb. No smoke coming from the vent-hole in the thatch, boards roughly nailed across the door and windows, and wantonly scattered around it all our little household belongings. Mutely they seemed to stare at me, telling me their story; a broken spinning-wheel, a cradle half embedded in the snow, a meal-kist deliberately emptied of its precious contents, a little wooden billet that had served for a child's toy.

But of my children there was not a sign. Only here and there the snow was trampled as if there had been a struggle.

Beating down my frenzy of rage and fear, I ran to our nearest neighbour. Since the last evictions, we had not been able to build as a community, but put up our houses where we could upon that terrible soil, and so my next neighbour was some distance from me. I crashed my fist upon his door, shouting to him, what had become of my children? He would not let me enter; he spoke to me through the hole that served for window in the turf wall.

'Man,' says he, trembling, 'messengers were sent all round the district, warning us under threat of similar treatment against giving shelter or assistance to wife, child, or animal belonging to Donald Macleod.'

'What are you?' I raged at him. 'Has your humanity deserted you altogether that you would keep your door closed against a woman and young children in their need?'

But he only shook his head at me, groaning out that he knew his house was watched, and that ruin would surely come upon him if he rendered assistance to me or mine. To such a pass had my race been driven, we of old so famous for our hospitality!

I did not stay to argue with him, but back I pelted to my own house, and searched about until I found some little tracks in the virgin snow, the footprints of children. So then I set off to follow them, dreading sore what I should find, fearing every moment to hear the scream of buzzards and the flapping of great wings gathering for a feast on all I held most dear.

The gale had blown itself out now, and a still breath of air, the very essence of winter, descended from the wild white heights of the hills, glazing the stepping-stones across a burn, crisping the snowdrifts, menacing with death from cold or slow starvation. Yet still I saw, deep in the white carpet, the pattern of toddling footsteps marching on before me.

Oh Donald Og! Donald Og! my little hero! Many a time have I wished since that day that I was a rich man, and could return to Scotland and raise a monument to your fame. I would build it as fine as ever mason built, and I would inscribe upon it in golden letters the epic of my lion-hearted son. In all the old stories I ever heard at our *ceilidhs*, of Fingal and his warriors, there was none to beat the heroism of a child not eight years old.

Does it come back to you, that deed of yours, as I recount the tale of it? Or have the mists of the long years made it faint? It is as clear to me, my son, as though I had been present.

You were sitting at the great-meal with your mother and your little sisters, while she nursed the infant on her lap. I think you did not hear the footsteps of doom approaching, because of the noise of wind and waves. Ay, all unprepared you must have been, when those eight men entered without knocking, and in a few brutal minutes tore up your childhood by the roots. My wife, in the few periods of sanity she enjoyed in after years, told me that their silence was the worst of all. It was as though they were indeed the ghosts she had seen in her vision, speaking no word, uttering no threat or insult; as one kills an insect, without fuss or emotion, so did these men desecrate my hearth.

First they turned you out, you, your mother, your sisters and the infant, and then they hurled after you all our bits of furniture, deliberately smashing it and emptying out our winter store of meal. The kettle simmering on its chain they tipped over on to the glowing peats, putting out the fire, and lastly they nailed boards across the door and windows. They went away as they had come, in silence.

There is a period of blank bewilderment, and then I hear you and your mother confer together, you the only man of the family in this black hour! You will stay here, you say stoutly, and take care of your little sisters and the baby, while your mother seeks shelter from a neighbour. For this is not as other evictions; only Donald Macleod and his family must go.

I fancy that I see you, dear heart, in your mother's long absence on this errand, collecting our scattered blankets and plaids to put up a kind of tent, and the gale tearing the stuff away from your small hands as fast as you gathered it. I see your mother returning, distraught, refused aid by her own kinsfolk, every door shut fast against her, they who were used to have a saying that if they closed their house against the merest stranger, Christ would shut them out from His eternal home.

What is to be done? The snow is beginning to fall fast; the night is coming. To stay here is to perish; aid must be got somewhere beyond the bounds of the estate, but your mother must seek it alone, for little legs cannot travel so far. I dare not follow her in my imagination as she sets off again, pursued by the wailing of your sisters and her babe.

No, no! I will set the eyes of my mind upon yourself, my hero! The blood of generations of brave ancestors stirred in your veins, and made you wise and valiant beyond your years. You were in charge! As the hours went by, you knew it was in vain to await the return of your poor mother; the slow cold hands of death were beginning to grope for the life of the infant, coming in the guise of sleep. I hear your childish voice rise dauntless above the crashing of the waves:

'Buckle up the baby on my back, and do you two take tight hold of me by the kilt!'

Was ever such a procession seen in history? Had ever little lad to face such a journey, not knowing whether, even could he make it, he would find succour? You had resolved to go to the house of your aunt Moir, a weary many miles away, and she with a husband as timid as a mouse. You would not forget to take provision with you; there was a bit of dried herring sticking out of the snow, and there was a scattering of oatmeal you could collect for your pocket. So off you set, a frail infant strapped on your back, two crying mites clutching at your skirts, their hands already numbing with the cold.

Often and often, Donald Og, I have gone with you in spirit on that dreadful journey. I have suffered with you the exhaustion, the crying need for sleep, the paralysing cramp of hunger, the bewilderment in your mind because of the human cruelty, more savage than a wolf's, that had driven you forth. I am telling you that I have been haunted in my dreams by your sudden stumble in the darkness, the slipping of your feet upon the treacherous ice; I have seen the gorge of the river yawning like a hungry mouth to swallow you, starvation stalking, a grim spectre, at your side, the mountains brooding over you, armed with avalanches, the bogs crackling and snarling beneath your wounded feet.

And yet I see you, head down-bent to watch each footstep, shoulders bowed beneath the living burden on your little back, grimly resolute, your feet daring the step that might spell death, your spirit defying the elements, your heart the tempting despair, the fibre of heroes answering stoutly the old challenge of aggression.

You were our race personified that night. You were Galgacus upon the Mount of Battle, you were Fingal driving back the Dane, you were Bruce's peasant army, determined to survive or else to go down fighting. In what you did there was that same unbending fortitude which caused Scotland's champion, William Wallace, to cry out to the Saxons who had captured him by a mean, base trick, 'Whatever power you have over my body, over my spirit you have none at all!'

I know that it must have been with the last of your childish strength that you struggled at length to the house of your aunt Moir, and, past speech, laid the infant in her lap. There I found you in the morning, who had never thought to look upon your face again.

16

LETTER FROM FACTOR GUNN TO
COMMISSIONER LOCH

FACTOR'S OFFICE, Farr, Sutherlandshire. June 15th, 1833.

I take the liberty, Sir, of sending you these few lines to inform you that at the long last the estate is rid of yon mischievous man and well-kent trouble-maker, Donald Macleod. I hope you'll be good enough to mention the fact to the noble proprietors, now their Graces, the Duke and Duchess of Sutherland.

I believed he would be away this last winter, which has been as hard a one in the Hielands as ever I remember, for I threatened all the sub-tenants in the neighbourhood against selling or giving him peats for his fire. But they let his wife take them underhand from their stacks, and Macleod having got masonry work at Thurso, he had plenty siller for his other necessities. I used my best endeavours to induce Mr Innes of Sandside to withdraw his protection from these squatters, but all I could say wouldna move him, so when Macleod was away at his work, I took the occasion of calling on his wife, and threatened her that if she didna instantly remove, I'd take steps that would astonish her.

I was obliged to repeat my warning several times, for the woman's clean daft and seemed not to understand what I said. But I hear the morn that she and her bairns flitted in the night-time, and are on their forty miles march to join Macleod at Thurso. You may rest assured, Sir, I'll take good care sic troublesome folk'll no venture back on any part of the estate.

17

EPILOGUE, 1883

THE old woman came slowly along the bridle-path, bent double from infirmity. Every now and then she would make short excursions into the wood at the side of the path, her little claw-like hands scrabbling among the grass and nettles to find some plant she wanted. She could not raise herself from this stooped posture, but often she would pause to listen with her head on one side, dreading to hear a Lowland voice shout, 'Keep tae the path, auld wifie, or ye'll disturb the deer!'

She was thirsty, and the music of a burn tempted her, but she dared not venture down to it. There might be a man-trap there. Away in the distance she heard the periodic banging off of guns, but she paid no attention. She had grown used to that sound during the past ten years.

Her fingers tightened on a root of wild liquorice, and now she began to tremble, for her hearing, still very acute for all her eighty-two years, had caught the snap of a twig far off along the path in the direction in which she was going. A keeper likely! She was doing no harm that she knew of, but that was just the trouble; you never knew nowadays what had become an offence. She had spent a few days in jail just for taking gulls' eggs from the rocks. There were footsteps audible now, approaching her at a swinging stride; she crouched down like a little animal among the undergrowth, hoping that the stranger would pass by without noticing that she was there.

But the footsteps halted when they were level with her; all

she could see was a pair of legs in worsted stockings and dusty boots. As she cowered, fearing some reprimand, a voice wished her good-morning in the Gaelic, and enquired the way to Strathy Point.

Her trembling increased, but now it was the shiver of a joy too great to be believed in. After a while she quavered:

'It is the voice of Donald Macleod. If my brother Donald is in life, you must be he.'

Two muscular arms came round her, the legs she had seen dropped on their knees, and a face was bent down to her level. She stared at it like one who sees a ghost. It was the face of a middle-aged man, tanned by a sun more powerful than ever shines in Britain, with a searching and resolute glance, and a look of constraint about the mouth.

'I am Donald Og, son of Donald Macleod, once of Strath Naver. Is it possible that you are my Aunt Moir, whom I have come across the ocean to visit?'

She could not answer. The ready tears of old age and weakness pattered down like rain upon the ground. He held her closely, rocking her like a baby, telling her that he had good news for her, that he had come all the way from Canada to bring it. It was as though he had said he had come from the moon.

The scenes of his early childhood bore little resemblance to the picture he had retained of them in his mind. There had been many new houses building then, of raw, bleak stone, and there had been hundreds of tiny turf cabins clinging to the sides of the cliffs. Now there was not a cabin to be seen, and only a few of the stone houses were occupied; others stood empty and in ruins, the wind rustling the rank grass and weeds which choked them, and whistling round a broken gable-end.

What had become of all the folk who had lived at Strathy Point? he enquired in astonishment. Moir shook her ancient head, and muttered that the young men and girls left the Highlands nowadays as soon as they were old enough either to emigrate or to find work in the towns; what was there to keep them in their native land any longer?

But those who remained came flocking to Moir's house to get a look at this visitant from another world, and to listen to the wonders he had to tell them. Their imagination boggled at the size of Canada—three million square miles of it, only a little less than the whole of Europe. And to get there it took but a fortnight in one of these mysteries called steamships. A new Scotland overseas, Donald Og named it, where the Gaelic was still spoken, and many of the old customs kept up, a country which had been largely colonised by Scotsmen, and where the senior settlers were the French, their ancient allies.

Of marvels incredible nearer home he told them. The railway ran all over Southern Scotland, and even as far north as Inverness; across the Tay there was a special bridge built for it. Ay, he had travelled by it, at thirty miles an hour, too, and for those who could afford it there was food to be bought while you were drawn along at such a speed, and some of the iron monsters had little beds with pillows. He showed them a box of friction matches, and frightened the younger children when he struck one to light his pipe; he said that some mad folk were flying in the air in balloons, that sportsmen rode about on a contraption called the bicycle, and that in America at anyrate you could talk to people miles and miles away through the telephone, invented by a Scotsman.

Young Mr David Mackenzie, the Minister, shook his head in disapproval. Such things, he said, were certainly of Satan.

But Donald Og had not made this long journey just to amuse his folk with wonders.

'There were three objects I had,' said he, 'that made me ask for leave of absence from my Colonel in the Royal Highland Emigrants. The first was to bring you some copies of my father's book; the second was to tell you some good news; and the third is something private, and only for the ears of my Aunt Moir.'

Donald Macleod's book! Donald Macleod an author! The little volume, badly printed and poorly bound, was passed from hand to hand, while those who could read English spelt out the title, *Gloomy Memories in the Highlands of Scotland*. There were not many left at Strathy Point who remembered Donald Macleod; those who did nodded their heads sagely, and said ach, Donald had always been the clever one at school. Since he had left Sutherland all those years ago, there had been vague rumours about him, and sometimes even a mention of his name in the newspapers, of how he had stood up at public meetings in Edinburgh and spoken fearlessly about his people's wrongs. Moir had maintained that he had actually got letters printed, though not signed with his name, but no one had quite credited that.

And now here was Donald Og, his eldest child, come to tell them the truth about it all. Not all the *ceilidhs* they had held in the old days, with the saga of Fingal retold about the peats, compared with these evenings when as many as could squeeze themselves into Moir's house heard the story of a humbler hero, one of their own clan, actually related to them by his son.

'All the sufferings that befell my father before he was driven from his native heath,' began Donald Og, 'only made him the more determined to publish the truth about the clearances. It was principally with this in mind that he settled in Edinburgh, where also he hoped that my poor mother's wits would return to her, when she was far from the scenes of such terror. Ochon! I well remember how she would flee whenever she saw a stranger approach, shrieking, "A ground-officer! He has come to turn us out!"'

'My father was confident of being able to maintain his family in the Lowlands, for he was very skilled with his hands. He did not know then that what had been well-paid labour, worth forty shillings a week, could now be done by children with the new machinery, and that a craftsman like himself would be lucky could he make three and sixpence a week at an uncreative, meaningless sequence of mechanical actions, terrible indeed to a man who was a master craftsman.

'It was my sisters and I who kept the pot boiling when first we moved to Edinburgh. Ay, and my poor mother. While she dragged a truck through the galleries of a coal-mine, with a chain passing between her legs and fastened to an iron waist-belt, my sisters tended machinery fourteen hours a day in a flax-mill, spending their Sabbaths cleaning the machines, and I sweated at a blast-furnace. Typhus, borne by lice, visited our slum dwelling yearly, and sent my mother and infant brother to their graves.

'My father, getting any work he could, never rested, never wavered from his resolution to write the story of the clearances. If I could tell you of all the obstacles he had to overcome! He was cold-shouldered by his companions in misery, the Lowland working men, who ridiculed him for his superior education and his polite manners; he was denied access to the ancient records of Scotland he wanted to consult for his story, for they are kept locked up in the Advocates' Library; and he was ignored altogether by those who professed to be the champions of the poor. The Lowlands had their own wrongs, and they would not trouble themselves about those of wild Highlandmen.

'Still my father kept his eyes fixed on his goal. He remembered very vividly the trial of Patrick Sellar and its outcome; often he would say to me as I grew older that Sellar and the landlords had the law on their side, and that what must be done was to rouse public opinion to the extent when there would be a demand for changing this unjust law.

'It was in 1840, seven long years after we had moved to the Lowlands, that my father won his first little triumph in that bitter fight of his. I was newly enlisted, and with my regiment in Afghanistan, so I missed being with my father on this great occasion. There was a meeting held in the British Hotel at Edinburgh to enquire into the miseries of the Highlands after a winter of dreadful famine, and it was decided by the proprietors and ministers who attended, that, so far as Sutherland was concerned, there was no need for public assistance, because the noble proprietor, the second Duke, could be relied upon to succour all on his estate.

'This was my father's chance. He wrote a letter to the *Edinburgh Weekly Journal*, setting forth his own experiences during the lifetime of his Grace's mother, and demanding that the cause and extent of the sufferings in his native place be made the subject of an impartial enquiry. This letter, which he signed "A Highlander", was published in the next issue of the *Journal* and caused a great sensation.

'But then there came a setback for my father. The same newspaper, while printing several letters accusing him of misrepresentation and ignorance, refused to publish his replies. I suppose the landlord influence had been brought to bear upon the Editor; at anyrate, my poor father was subjected to much scorn among his acquaintances, for deserting his cause on the one hand, and of failing to substantiate his charges on the other.

'Yet he would not yield, not he! There were other newspapers, and by and bye he induced the *Edinburgh Weekly Chronicle* to give him a hearing, ay, and to publish no less than twenty-five long letters from his pen. Those were the brief good days, right enough! When I heard from him at long intervals he was exultant; at last his perseverance was rewarded, he was exposing avarice and oppression, he was doing something for our ancient Gaelic race. He was encouraged not only by the public interest he was arousing, but by the multitude of letters he received confirming all he had written, though many of the writers begged to remain anonymous, for fear of reprisals.

'But if you have money and influence, there are ways of muzzling the mouth of the Press. When he took his next letter to the office of the newspaper, my father was told that the *Edinburgh Weekly Chronicle* had failed, and had closed its doors.

'I think he must have been as near despair that day as his stout heart would let him. Just when his struggles for a hearing seemed to be bearing fruit, his pen was silenced.

And all the time there were new injustices to be exposed.

'In the winter of 1846, the great potato famine brought starvation to the Highlands, as some of you may remember to your cost. Boards of Relief were set up by the Government in London, at which our poor folk were miscalled "indolent and intractable characters, enemies to progress and improvement, dirty lazy savages who will do nothing to help themselves if they can get charity". Hence it was decreed that no man or woman in the Highlands was to be relieved by the public subscriptions without working for it; and to test their real need of relief there were officials sent amongst them, little better than spies, who, after prying into all their circumstances, were empowered to offer one pound of meal for ten hours' labour, with the addition of half a pound for those who had children too young to toil.

'But even this was not the worst of it, for it was decided that those Highland proprietors who had been generous enough to subscribe to the Relief Fund were the best able to judge who among their people needed assistance, and were the proper persons to distribute it. Thus these noble landlords got great sums into their hands.

'Our Duke of Sutherland, who had subscribed two thousand pounds, got six thousand to distribute among his starving people, and proceeded to lay out some of this gold in building himself a splendid hunting-lodge on his estate, and a road of thirty miles leading to it, solely for his own convenience. It is true he spent the remainder on meal, which of course he entrusted to the factors; and I need not tell you who were the sufferers, how much of it was kept in their possession until it was thrown in rotten blue lumps into the sea.

'Only perhaps you do not know that when accountants were employed to examine the books of the Relief Board, they found between six and seven thousand pounds unaccounted for, and that the affair had to be hushed up to avoid a public scandal.

'Away went my father's pen once more, away his slender

means on ink and paper. "I have been peeled and plucked so often," he wrote to me, "that I have scarcely a feather left in my wings, but I will be at them again until I have won a hearing, and have convinced all honest men throughout Great Britain that Highland landlords are the guilty authors of this and former distress and famine, and not the good God, as the ministers blasphemously maintain, nor my poor people."

'But now I had received a grant of land in Canada, such as was promised to all of my regiment after ten years' service, and I had set up a good farm there. I wrote my father imploring him to come out to me, to spend the evening of his days in the new Scotland, which has the sense of nationhood our old one has lost. I told him I was sure that I could get influential gentlemen to publish his letters in the form of a book if he would come. It was this last inducement, I am certain, that persuaded him to tear up his roots and cross the sea.

'Sure enough, he found plenty good folk over there ready to assist him, and to encourage him to go on setting down in what he has always called his plain, unvarnished style the story of the Sutherland Clearances. Ay, this litttle book that I have brought to you may be found in the libraries of great rich men in Canada, as well as on the home-made shelves of the poor.

'And that is not the end of it. My father, in extreme old age, has got a hearing on this side of the Atlantic. Some residents of Greenock republished his old letters privately, and they reached the hands of a learned and fearless gentleman, Mr Alastair Mackenzie, the Editor of the *Celtic Magazine*. What must Mr Mackenzie do but write a book himself, entitled *The History of the Highland Clearances*, in which he has included not only all that my father ever wrote, but a reprint of the trial of Patrick Sellar, with some very strong comments on the partiality of the Judge and the packing of the jury. My word! such a stir this has made throughout the length and breadth of Great Britain that there has been set up a Royal Commission to make impartial enquiry into the grievances of our poor Highland folk.

'When news of this reached me in Canada I could not rest until I had come over to discover for myself what would be done for those who are my people. I have spoken with a gentleman who sits on this Commission and he has assured me that there will be an Act of Parliament passed as a result of its findings, giving security of tenure and compelling our landlords to reduce their rents. And he told me also that, even so early, he has formed the opinion from his investigations that, "In no part of His Majesty's dominions are there to be found, among the humbler ranks of society, more intelligence, better manners or purer morals, than among the Scottish Highlanders." We who have always been vilified as dirty, idle savages!

'Is this not the good news that's in it?' concluded Donald Og triumphantly. 'You will have justice done to you at last, and maybe you will even be permitted to return to Strath Naver, and have your good crofts as in the old days of which my father has so often told me. Through all my travels in the Highlands I have seen but very few sheep; surely they have been cleared away to make room for men once more. If there is justice in this world, it must be so.'

The eyes about the fireside circle gazed at him, dim, patient eyes of old men and women, the wondering stare of children. They were idle as they listened; no longer was there wool to card or spin; the comfort of snuff or tobacco was only a dim memory. They listened as to some fairy-tale, something that entertained but did not really concern their everyday lives.

'Well, look at that now!' they murmured. 'That's a wonderful thing whatever!'

A curious delicacy of feeling prevented them from hurting Donald Og's kind heart, from damping his enthusiasm, by telling him the truth about the sheep.

They did not quite understand it themselves, only that it had something to do with a new land called Australia, so they had heard, whence wool and carcases came over by the shipload. At anyrate, the second Duke of Sutherland had cleared his estate of shepherds and collies and black-faced sheep, even as his father had cleared it of human beings, and had put two million acres under that which had become a more valuable creature, the red-deer.

Some of the old folk grew reminiscent. They remembered the funeral of the first Duke, the very year he got his new honour. Ay, the ministers had ordered a strict fast to be kept, though it was in the very middle of the herring season, when to be idle was to fail in one's rent; and they had all been compelled to subscribe to a handsome monument in Dornoch Cathedral, setting forth his Grace's virtues. And then a few years later (in 1839, was it?), his wife the Duchess had followed him to the grave, and was buried with the rites of the Church of England. Ay, she would be ashamed of her Scots blood even in death. Patrick Sellar had written a great long poem on her in some paper.

They shivered. Even now that name was ominous.

Bent over the fire, blinking at its red heart, Moir had listened more to the voice than to the words of Donald Og's story. It was her brother's voice, familiar, long cherished in her heart, evoking a host of tender memories; the words, though spoken in 'the language', had made little sense to her. She was pleased when she understood that perhaps the younger folk would be freed from the threat of eviction for ever brooding over them, and might have their rents reduced, those rents for which one had to depend nowadays on the sons and daughters who had gone out into the world beyond the mountains, where it was still possible to earn money.

But she would never live to see such things, for dimly she comprehended that the fine gentlemen who ruled in the South took time enough when it came to passing Acts of

Parliament designed to relieve folk, though in the matter of removals and evictions their swiftness was terrible indeed. She did not complain; silent endurance was a virtue she had inherited from her father, and if she could grow a few sticks of kale, and a little row of potatoes, sufficient to keep body and soul together, she was content. And besides there were wild herbs and roots to be gathered if you kept your eyes upon the ground, as her infirmity had obliged her to do for many years. Ay, the rheumatism was a blessing in disguise.

In the same vague way she was proud of her brother Donald. A great fighter he was, and always had been, with the spirit of their mother in him. But what Moir understood completely, and what really roused her to action, was the third purpose of her nephew's visit, a purpose he confided to her alone.

'My father,' he told her, 'has long felt death approaching, and there is a last boon that he craves. Though he cannot be buried with the dust of his ancestors in his native soil, he longs that there may be in his grave, under skies which must be for ever alien to him, a handful of earth from Strath Naver.'

'I will be fetching it for you tomorrow,' said Moir emphatically.

No, she would not have Donald Og accompany her on the long walk to her old home. He would find some sort of conveyance for her? For what reason had the good Lord given her legs if it were not to walk? she demanded. She would manage fine; she knew how to avoid the game-keepers, going as she did constantly about the countryside to gather roots and fungi for cooking, and herbs for medicines. And she had clear in her mind just the spot where their original home had stood; Donald should have his handful of earth from the very place where he had heard his first lullaby.

She had long grown used to the desolate aspect of what had once been the clachan of Rossal. Sometimes in her fancy she put back the houses and peopled them with ghosts, but with her bodily eyes she could see only strange hummocks in the ground marking the foundation stones of cottages, an unevenness where the run-rigs had been, a few tumbled stones, long overgrown with moss and lichen, where the mill of the district had stood.

But today she was disconcerted to find Rossal occupied. The first she knew of it was to see some delicate skeins of blue smoke going up into the autumn air, a parody of the old homely peat-reek that used to issue from a hundred hearths. For a moment she wondered whether she had strayed into the world of spirits; but then some setters and retrievers barked at her, and she smelt the aroma of expensive cigars. A party of gentlemen on a grouse-drive had selected this spot to eat their luncheon, part of a broken mill-stone making a fine back-rest for them in the sun.

One of them spied Moir, and called out sharply to the beaters, who sat respectfully apart beside the ponies, their panniers bulging with spoil:

'If that filthy old crone attempts to beg, turn her off directly, do you hear?'

But the aged woman did not venture near the party. Her grotesque little figure in its shapeless garments went rooting among the hummocks, and the sportsmen, forgetting her, continued to eat cold salmon and salad, chatting pleasantly as they passed round a silver flask.

'I believe, you know, that this Bonny Strathnaver is the site of the most famous of the Sutherland clearances, for which, whatever their grandfathers may have been, the present generation is not sufficiently grateful. The migration to the sea-coast was designed solely for the purpose of adding the resources of the ocean to those of their crofts. I have just been reading an interesting book on the subject, by a Mr Thomas Sellar, whose father, I understand, was once Factor of the estate. The present smiling aspect of this their late habitation is due, not to any relics of their industry, but to the reclamations carried out so extensively by the sheep-farmers who succeeded them.'

'They, I mean the peasants, are the most surly and rapacious fellows I have ever come across. The able-bodied go off to the herring-ports for ten weeks every year, where they can earn as much as twenty-five pounds sterling. Yet they haggle over selling us a lobster for our table!'

'Their excuse for everything is land-hunger, a most infectious disease, as we have seen to our cost in Ireland, and men will always listen to those who tell them they are ill-used. But the trouble with the Scotch Highlanders is an engrained determination to be idle. I hear that our recruiting-sergeants get less and less volunteers from these parts every year.'

'Well, *we* have not been idle this morning! Twenty-four brace of grouse, eight hares, and a woodcock! Bless my soul, though the Duke charges pretty steep for his shooting rights, it is worth it when he has made such a paradise for sportsmen.'

One member of the party had taken no part in this conversation, but had been jealously watching the old woman. From time she stopped and bent over her poke, in which she seemed to be secreting something.

This gentleman was a dilletante, dabbling in half a dozen different hobbies, and sadly boring his friends with his enthusiasms. While eating his luncheon he had discoursed at large on chambered cairns and tumuli, on brochs and flint arrowheads, honestly convinced that he was being both entertaining and instructive. Now he suddenly began to describe a harrowing experience he had suffered yesterday.

'Having discovered a considerable vein of pumice and vitreous scoriae in that exceedingly fearsome eminence they call the Mountain of the Maiden, or some such fanciful name, I collected a bagful of specimens which I gave to a native whom I met, bidding him carry it by a short cut over the hills to my inn, while I went by the road. What was my mortification when, on opening the bag, I found that all my precious specimens had disappeared, and that the bag now contained common stones.'

His companions murmured polite sympathy.

'Addressing myself to my porter, I demanded an explanation. "I thought it was a wonderful thing whatever," says he, "why the bag should be so dreadfully heavy, so I opened it, and finding it filled with stones I emptied them out. But I have filled the bag again from the cairn beside the inn, sir, and I have given you good measure for your money." The appalling ignorance of these savages! And now supposing that this aged crone has lighted on some rare plant without knowing it. I really must go and see what she is up to. It is distressing to think that I should return from my Scotch holiday having missed some treasure.'

'Augustus should have been born a terrier,' chuckled one of his companions, as the enthusiast hurried off. 'I never knew a man to be so fond of digging.'

The other members of the party smilingly agreed, congratulating themselves on the fact that they, at least, had missed nothing. They had killed every creature they saw on legs and wings, on land and sea; they had bagged a seal, which was now on its way to London to make a snug lining for a greatcoat, and a pole-cat which was to be stuffed and put into a glass case. When there was nothing more exciting, they had kept their hands in by banging away at the gulls and hoodie-crows.

One of them, pleasantly relaxed, and expansive after several pulls at the silver flask, now delivered a little lecture on the fine art of sending grouse so that they would arrive fresh at their destination.

'You must sprinkle pepper liberally in his beak and under his wings, and wherever else there is evidence of heavy shot marks. Then roll his head up in kitchen paper, slip it under his wing, fold him up so that some part of the paper goes between his other wing and his breast, twist the end off at his tail, and lay him in the box. Put him and his *compagnons de voyage* heads and tails, a few sprigs of nice fresh heather on top, and nail the lid down. So will you be complimented by the grateful recipients upon the condition in which your birds have reached them. I have known many a reputation made by learning so simple an art!'

He yawned. It was fantastic to reflect that no later than next Monday the railway would ensure he once again had his feet under his desk, and his energies directed upon the London Stock Market.

'Shall you come up again for the stalking?' one of his friends enquired.

'Yes, indeed. I arranged it with the Duke's Factor last week. (By gad, his Grace must make a pretty penny from the wild-life on his estate here! I understand that our American cousins have cottoned on to our sport, as they say, and that Dunrobin Castle, so elegantly rebuilt by the late Duke, is let to some rich Yankee.) I hope to get that splendid antlered fellow I missed last season, and all through my foolish friend, Lord Longton, who lit a cigar just when the gillies were driving the deer towards the muzzles of our guns. Of course my antlered quarry soon snuffed the aroma and retreated to his cavern.'

'Well, tomorrow is Sunday, our day of rest,' summed up a gentleman with luxuriant whiskers. 'Very welcome after a hot week, and such hard work.'

The dilletante, meanwhile, was picking his way round a patch of bog in the direction of Moir, puffing a little, for he was loaded with paraphernalia, a box of water-colours, a killing-bottle for butterflies, a magnifying-glass, and endless notebooks.

'What have you got there, my good woman?' he demanded, when he came within earshot.

She had been on her knees, grubbing away at a hummock, but at the sound of a voice she raised herself as far as her infirmity would allow and cowered from the stranger, clutching against her breast a shabby little poke she had been filling.

'Give it to me and let me see what you have got,' commanded the enthusiast, his curiosity aroused. And then, as she only shrank further from him, he took out his purse and held up a shilling. 'Come, old dame, you don't see many of these bright coins, I am confident, and it shall be yours just for a peep into that bag you are holding.'

To his extreme chagrin, Moir turned her back on him and went scuttling away up the strath, for all the world like a little wild animal, still clutching her mysterious treasure. Should he go after her? But no, he could scarcely use force on a female; and besides, she was probably verminous. But he was very annoyed, as he dropped the rejected shilling back into his purse. It would be good, after all, to return to civilisation, to the noble profession of banking, to gas lights and the rumble of traffic, even to the swarms of beggars on the London streets, who at least were grateful if you threw them a halfpenny, and cried, 'Gawd bless you, kind gen'le-man!', instead of taking offence like these proud Highland paupers.

There was something eerie about that permanently bowed figure, he thought, staring after Moir. He gave an involuntary shiver, wondered whether he had caught a chill, and sensibly resolved to take his night-cap of whisky piping hot before retiring to bed. It was pleasant to reflect that he was staying tonight, not at the inn, but at the ornate shooting-lodge (which had arisen, had he but known it, on the site of Captain Gordon's house), with the powdered flunkeys staring in boredom through the windows, and the expensive odour of game turning high in the cellars.

For come to think of it, there was an uncanniness about this "Bonny Strathnaver", now that the dusk was falling. He was a man devoted to solitary pursuits, and therefore was apt to grow a little fanciful at times.

Evening was spreading grey wings across the sky, and all colour had faded from the velvet slopes of the hills, leaving only a faint stain on the heather, the colour of old blood. It seemed to the enthusiast that the great bens were closing in upon the strath, putting out gnarled hands like feelers, and that the voice of the river was suddenly loud and hungry. The mists boiling out of the gullies might so easily be mistaken, by a sensitive man, for a company of ghosts, returning by night to sit about old hearthstones.

Slowly, silently, they descended, mingling with other wraiths that came wavering up from the river. It was only some trick of the breeze, of course, that made them seem to form into a straggling procession, and to follow in the tracks of the little bowed figure, like an escort guarding one who bore a treasure to some unknown destination, over the hills and far away.